Between Two Packs

Emily Walters

Between Two Packs

Published by Emily Walters

Copyright © 2019 by Emily Walters

ISBN 978-1-07487-332-5

First printing, 2019

All rights reserved. No part of this book may be reproduced in any form or by any electronic or mechanical means including information storage and retrieval systems – except in the case of brief quotations in articles or reviews – without the permission in writing from its publisher, Emily Walters.

www.EmilyWaltersBooks.com

PRINTED IN THE UNITED STATES OF AMERICA

Dedication

I want to dedicate this book to my beloved husband, who makes every day in my life worthwhile. Thank you for believing in me when nobody else does, giving me encouragement when I need it the most, and loving me simply for being myself.

Table of Contents

CHAPTER 1 1

CHAPTER 2 10

CHAPTER 3 19

CHAPTER 4 29

CHAPTER 5 41

CHAPTER 6 51

CHAPTER 7 58

CHAPTER 8 70

CHAPTER 9 78

CHAPTER 10 92

CHAPTER 11 111

CHAPTER 12 122

CHAPTER 13 132

EPILOGUE 141

WHAT TO READ NEXT? 145

ABOUT EMILY WALTERS 148

ONE LAST THING...149

Chapter 1

Kayla took a deep, calming breath. Her heart raced and her hands shook a little as she raised a fist and knocked on the door three times. She heard a muffled voice curse, then shuffling feet approaching the door.

She shifted her suitcase to her other hand. She shouldn't feel this nervous about seeing her own father. For a split second, she considered jumping back into her navy-blue Honda and tearing out of the driveway, away from the tiny New York town where she'd been born and raised. Where would she go? She wasn't sure. She wanted to see her father again, but she didn't know if she could stand it if he yelled at her, or brought up the argument they'd had on the day she'd left for college—or worse, if he said nothing and slammed the door in her face.

Would he even want to see her again? She tried to convince herself that coming back home hadn't been a huge mistake, and only half succeeded.

The hinges squealed as he eased the door open and peered out. Her heart leaped in her chest, both in joy and dismay.

It had been four years since she'd seen him last, and he'd changed. His hair, once the same thick, luxurious brown as her own, was now almost completely white. His arms were no longer the thick slabs of bristling muscle they'd been her entire life. They were draped in sagging skin, and he was beginning to develop a beer gut. His eyes were red and bleary, but in their depths she caught a glimpse of the same hard light that she recognized from her childhood.

Shock flickered across Mark Hudson's face.

Kayla smiled. Her mouth was dry. "Hi, Daddy."

He said nothing for what seemed like an eternity. A bird trilled in the distance and a squirrel chattered in the oak tree in front of his cabin, the same tree from which she'd hung dozens of tire swings and, once, fallen and broken her arm. The silence was almost unbearable.

Finally, he swung the door open and, wordlessly, enveloped her in a crushing hug.

Tears stung her eyes. Had he forgiven her, then, for the horrible way she'd acted before she'd left?

"Kayla," he said, his voice muffled against her shoulder. "I can't believe…I mean, I'm so glad to see you again."

"Me too, Daddy," she said. They finally pulled apart. She noticed that her father's eyes were also a little watery.

"What are you doing here?" He was still smiling, but she noticed the slight note of suspicion in his voice.

Kayla shifted her feet. "I graduated two weeks ago."

"Oh." He looked slightly sheepish. "Graphic design, right?"

"Yes. Anyway, I thought I'd come see you for a little bit before I got my own place. I'm sorry I didn't invite you to my graduation." Her cheeks blazed with shame. "In fact, I'm sorry for everything. I was wrong, the way I treated you."

She could tell by the clear pain in his eyes that he, too, was remembering the last time they'd seen each other. The screaming match had been awful; he didn't want her to go to school two states away, and she'd accused him of suffocating her with his controlling, overbearing ways. It wasn't until she'd grown and matured that she'd realized that maybe he had a good reason. She'd been a stubborn, headstrong child, after all, and after her mother had died when she was thirteen, she was all the family that Mark had left. It was only natural for him to feel overprotective, and if he hadn't always exactly shown that he'd had her best interests at heart, that wasn't entirely his fault.

"I'm sorry, too," he said. He cleared his throat and hesitated. Kayla knew that apologies weren't Mark's strong suit, they never had been. "I shouldn't have tried to stop you from living your life."

"I'm just sorry that I never tried to talk to you sooner," Kayla said softly. "I've always regretted it."

Wrinkles popped up around her father's eyes as he smiled. "You're here now. That's all that matters." He threw the door open wide, and Kayla felt the last of the awkwardness between them melt away. "Come on in."

She followed her father through the hallway, dragging her suitcase behind her. She took a deep breath, inhaling scents that reawakened her memories of childhood—leather, varnish, wood smoke, and coffee. She hadn't realized just how badly she'd missed her father and her old home until she'd returned.

The cabin was small but cozy. Mark had built it himself shortly before Kayla was born, and until she'd left for college, she hadn't lived anywhere else.

For a moment Kayla's vision doubled, and she saw herself at eight years old, playing with her dolls in the middle of the floor while her mother laughed, her eyes alight and her cheeks glowing. Then Kayla blinked and just like that the illusion was gone—she was twenty-two, her father was old and feeble, and her mother was dead. A deep, searing ache settled around her heart. Where had the time gone?

Mark shuffled over to the kitchen. Kayla noticed that he was limping slightly.

"What happened to your leg?" she inquired as she sank into the brown leather armchair, the one that had been her favorite for years.

Mark grunted as he came back and sat down on the sofa across from her. He tossed her a can of Coke, and she cracked it open and drank gratefully. It had been a long drive, and she'd been dying for a soda. "Nothing in particular, it just twinges now and again," he said shortly.

She studied his face, and a real flash of unease ran through her as she noted the pain lines etched around his mouth and his eyes. "Are you okay?" she asked timidly.

Mark took a long, deep swallow of his beer. "Never better." But he avoided her eyes, and she had the distinct feeling that he was lying to her.

Kayla shifted uncomfortably in her seat. "Are you sure?"

"Yes." This time there was no mistaking the coldness in his voice, and he'd made it clear to her that the subject was closed. She wanted to press him further anyway, pester him until he told her exactly just how bad his health was, but before she could, he changed the subject.

"How long did you say you were staying?"

She fiddled with her drink. "Well, I'd like to stay for the summer. I'd start applying for jobs in New York

City around July and leave in late August, so a couple of months." She looked up. "Is that okay?" she added uncertainly.

His eyes softened. "You don't have to ask me. You're welcome here as long as you'd like to stay."

The silence that followed wasn't quite uncomfortable—Mark was a man of few words, and Kayla was used to passing entire evenings without saying more than a handful of words. She didn't mind.

"How's Uncle Emerson doing?" she finally inquired.

Mark brightened a little bit. "Good. Really good. He asks about you all the time, you know. You should go see him one of these days."

"I will," Kayla promised. Emerson wasn't her real uncle, but her father's best friend had been a steady figure in her life ever since she'd been a little girl, and she loved him like an uncle.

"Are any of your old friends still in town?"

Kayla sighed. "Not many. Becca and Maddie have both left. Julie's in college a couple of towns over and probably won't have time to hang out. Natalie's still here, but she has three kids now and their father took off, so she's working two jobs to support them. I probably won't be able to see her, either."

"Thank God I never had to worry about you getting knocked up that young," Mark said. "You beat teenage pregnancy, Kayla. How's it feel?"

She laughed, a belly-deep laugh that caused her shoulders to shake and tears to gather in her eyes. It was a good laugh, and instantly she felt better. "Feels pretty good."

The time flew by like lightning, and when Kayla glanced up at the clock, she was startled to see that it was already ten o'clock. Ever since the initial silence, she and her father had talked almost non-stop—reliving old memories, catching up on the events of the past four years, and laughing more than she'd laughed in a long time. She wished she'd come home sooner. It would have saved her a lot of guilt.

Mark stood, wincing. "Well, I guess I better be headed to bed."

"Do you have to go to work in the morning?"

He blinked, looking a little confused. It scared her to see her father, her strong, sure, stoic father, look like that. "What? Oh, no. I'm retired, Kayla."

"Oh." Her cheerful mood was gone, popped like a bubble. As long as they were talking and she didn't think about it too much, it was all too easy to imagine that things had never really changed. She couldn't remember a time when her father didn't work at the auto shop. Hell, he'd worked there her whole life.

Without his work, what did he do all day? Was he even the same person? Just how much had he changed while she'd been off doing her own thing? Guilt and a deep, undefinable sorrow burned in her heart.

"Where can I sleep?"

He gave her a crooked little smile, and it, at least, hadn't changed. "I kept your loft the way you left it. I haven't been up since you left. Everything still should be there."

She beamed. "Really?" Some of her happiness came rushing back. The loft, which had been part bedroom and part playroom, had been her absolute favorite place when she was a child.

"Really." His eyes sparkled, giving off an illusion of health and youth.

They hugged then, and she could feel his stubble tickling her cheek. "Thank you for coming home," he said in her ear.

She squeezed his hands as they pulled apart, and that seemed to be all the response he needed.

As he retired to his room, Kayla crossed over to the ladder in the hallway and cautiously climbed up. She was a slender girl, but she still weighed several pounds more than she had the last time she'd been up in the loft.

Except for a clear inch of dust, it was exactly the same as she remembered. The walls were pink with lavender trim, and her bed was heaped with pillows. Boxes stood in one corner—all of her clothes and toys that she'd gathered up one day when she was sixteen to be taken to the Salvation Army. But she'd never had the heart to get rid of them.

Now, she spent an hour poring through the boxes, handling her dolls and racecars and stuffed animals and toy guns (she'd never been particular about her toys, and had always had a tomboyish streak to match her girly side) but most of all, reliving and savoring her old, half-forgotten memories.

Chapter 2

"Do you need anything from the store?"

Mark glanced up from his newspaper. "No, I'm good."

"You sure?"

"Yeah," he said absently. He took a bite of cereal, still staring intently at the morning paper lying neatly on the table.

She jingled her keys in her hand and watched her father sharply. It had been a week since she'd come home, and gradually Mark had sunk into a surly, silent mood…when he was actually home, that is. Several times he just seemed to disappear, and last night, she hadn't heard him come in at all—she didn't know when he'd finally come home, but it had to have been past two o'clock, when she'd finally given up waiting for him and gone to bed. She was worried about him, but no amount of badgering or concerned questions would persuade him to tell her what was going on.

"I'll be back in a little bit, then."

"Hold on." He turned his head. Purplish shadows were beginning to bloom under his eyes and he was in dire need of a shave. "You're just going to Youngstown, right?"

"No, I thought I'd drive a little further and go to Lewiston. They have a Dunkin' Donuts."

His eyes narrowed. "I don't want you going there by yourself."

She raised her eyebrows. The cabin was located in a patch of woodland on the outskirts of Youngstown, which was a tiny, cozy little town. Lewiston was much larger, but it wasn't a dangerous place, and it was only ten miles away.

"Why? You think I'm going to get mugged or something?" She was aware of the sarcasm in her voice, but she was powerless to stop it.

He set his glass of orange juice down with more force than he'd intended; it slopped over the side. "Kayla, that's final."

She closed her eyes and counted backwards from ten. Finally, she calmed down. She wouldn't lose her cool again with her father, not after finally patching things up with him. She was older and wiser now, and she wasn't going to butt heads with him over something stupid. "Okay, Daddy."

He looked momentarily startled, as if he'd already prepared a counterargument and now had no cause to use it. "All right then," he said sheepishly.

She smiled a little. She'd discovered a way to stop Mark right in his tracks.

Still, she felt sort of guilty as she climbed into her car and started the engine. She didn't like lying to her father, but he'd left her no choice, really. She wasn't a child, after all, and she didn't see any harm in driving to Lewiston on a Saturday morning.

Besides, she really wanted donuts.

Fifteen minutes later she was waiting in line, breathing in the delicious aroma of coffee and cinnamon. Her mouth watered, and she anxiously shifted in place.

Hurry up, she thought irritably. The people in line were taking their sweet time ordering the food. Her stomach growled.

Preoccupied as she was, at first she didn't notice the man in front of her. He was tall, six feet at least, and his white T-shirt clung to his back and his broad, muscular shoulders. A tribal tattoo peeked out from underneath his left sleeve, and his dark hair was tousled and slightly curly.

He was throwing her glances over his shoulder, and as she caught a glimpse of his rugged, handsome face, her stomach swooped pleasantly. He was obviously checking her out.

Kayla nervously checked her reflection in the window and finger-combed her long brown hair, which she'd only half-heartedly run a brush through on her way out the door. She was wearing faded, torn jeans and an old tank top that had definitely seen better days, and not a drop of makeup. *The one day I walk out of the house looking like garbage and I see a hot guy. Figures,* she thought glumly.

There was no mistaking the interest in his eyes, but the second that they locked with hers, he looked hastily away.

She frowned. Maybe he was just shy. Either way, after three more times, she couldn't stand it anymore and tapped him on the shoulder.

"Hi," she said, and her wide smile quickly evaporated, replaced by hurt confusion.

He shot her a withering look and his upper lip twitched, as if she were something vile and disgusting. He didn't say a word and turned back around. His shoulders were rigid, as if he were tense, and he didn't look back.

Her cheeks flamed—she could almost feel the heat radiating from her face. God, that was embarrassing. She supposed she'd mistaken his interested glances for something else.

Her humiliation quickly turned to anger. Okay, she'd obviously been mistaken, but there was absolutely no need for him to be a snob about it. Her joy in the day was gone, and she glowered at the young man's back as if she could burn holes in his shirt with the pure power of her resentment alone.

He finally reached the counter.

"The usual, Adam?" the perky blond cashier asked.

"Yeah," Adam said as he plunked his money down in front of her. She busied herself making his coffee and passed it to him in a Styrofoam cup.

He turned around, his hands full, and shot Kayla a look that dripped with contempt. And fear? Was it possible? Before she could analyze it, he was gone.

So was her appetite. She ordered anyway, but her taste for donuts had disappeared.

"What's the deal with that guy?" she asked the cashier.

The blond girl passed a full bag of donuts to Kayla. "Who, Adam?"

"Yeah. He kept looking at me funny."

"Don't let it bother you. He can be a little surly, but he's really a sweet guy. He's from around here, so I see him in here a lot."

"I bet," Kayla said absently. She gave the cashier her money. "Thanks."

As she strode across the half-full parking lot, Kayla caught another glimpse of Adam, this time behind the wheel of a sleek black Jag. He didn't see her as he pulled out of the driveway, and again Kayla noticed just how strikingly handsome he was—when his face wasn't contorted in a sneer, that was.

She shook her head and climbed into her car.

While she drove, she tried not to think about Adam. Thinking about the way he'd looked at her sent a chill down her spine.

A short while later, she swung open the front door. Mark glanced up. "That took a while."

"Yeah, sorry about that. There was a huge line at the 7-Eleven."

His eyes narrowed and he crossed his arms. "Then why are you holding a Dunkin' Donuts bag?"

Crap. Her plan had been to eat in the car and throw the bag away before she came home, but her encounter with Adam had completely driven it from her mind. "Oh, that."

"Yes, that." His eyes flashed with anger. "Kayla, did you go to Lewiston?"

"Yeah," Kayla grumbled. There was no sense in trying to lie her way out of it now.

"So you lied to me?"

"I'm sorry."

Mark threw his hands in the air, exasperated. "Did you ever stop to think that I had a perfectly good reason for not wanting you to go there?"

"I guess not."

"Of course you didn't." His voice was gaining pitch, which Kayla knew from experience was a bad sign. She had to calm him down soon, otherwise he'd wind himself up for a full-blown argument, and the last thing she wanted was to put additional strain on their relationship. "You never—"

"I'm sorry, and it won't happen again."

He paused, his formerly muscular chest heaving. A muscle in his face jumped, as if he were just itching to add something to the conversation. Finally, he sighed.

"You're an adult now. I can't expect for you to follow orders from me anymore." Suddenly he looked almost anguished. "But please, please believe me when I say that you must not go back there again, not without me around."

She raised her eyebrows. What could possibly be so dangerous about Lewiston?

"I promise."

His shoulders relaxed. "Good." He looked at her sharply. "Did anything happen while you were in town?"

"No, why?"

He ignored her question. "Nothing at all?"

"Unless you count some guy giving me the evil eye in the Dunkin' Donuts line."

"What did he look like?"

She stared at him. "Are you serious?"

"Yes," he said impatiently.

Kayla blew a sigh. "Tall. Dark hair. Maybe a year or two older than me. He had a tattoo on his shoulder."

Mark jumped a little, as if he'd been electrocuted. "Did he say anything to you? Follow you, maybe?"

Kayla's eyes widened, and for a split second she feared that her father was losing his mind. "No. What on earth's gotten into you?" For at that moment Mark had leapt up and limped to the living room window, where he was now peering through the blinds at the driveway, as if he were expecting someone to pull up at any moment.

Mark whirled around. His hair was sticking up in corkscrews and he was still unshaven. "You can't go back to Lewiston," he repeated.

Kayla crossed her arms. "Are you going to tell me what's going on? Who was that guy, and why do you think I'm in danger?"

Mark ignored her and sank down on the couch. He began flipping through channels, although his eyes were glazed and far away, as if he wasn't seeing the screen.

A pulse beat at Kayla's temple. Nothing had changed. She'd been foolish to believe otherwise. Here she was, at twenty-two years old, and her father was still treating her like a teenager. She loved her father with all her heart, but God forgive her, he could drive her insane. Didn't she deserve to know why he was acting this way?

She blew a sigh and stalked off to her bedroom, which she'd cleaned from top to bottom and now carried the pleasant aroma of scented candles and furniture polish instead of dust and age. She flopped down on her bed.

Mark wasn't the only one with a stubborn streak. She'd find out what was going on.

So thinking, she slipped into a thin, uneasy doze.

Chapter 3

Kayla waited patiently for her father to catch up. Mark was limping worse than ever and the grimace on his face was pronounced. His pain was especially bad today, although he'd waved her away when she'd suggested that they stay home. "No way I'm passing up an opportunity to go fishing," he'd declared.

She'd known better than to try and persuade him otherwise. Still, she didn't like the way he looked.

She shifted her fishing pole to her other hand as he finally reached the small boat. "Think they'll bite?"

"I sure hope so. I'd hate to have gone all the way out here for nothing."

The weeks had slipped by, and warm May had given away to a hot, dry June. With each passing day, Kayla feared that her father was slipping further and further away from her. Ever since the incident at Lewiston, Kayla's relationship with her father had become even more strained. He was beginning to get irritated with her constant questions about his health and where he was disappearing to for long periods of time. She, in turn, was fed up with his behavior, and they were spending an increasing amount of time sitting in silence.

But she'd never regretted coming back. She might clash with him, but she loved him, and she was determined not to shut him out of her life again. So that morning she'd suggested that they go fishing, and she knew that it had been a good idea; already she could feel the tension between them melting away. It was something they'd done together a lot when she was a kid, even more so after her mother's death. Fishing had helped them both cope.

They climbed into the shallow aluminum fishing boat, which was streaked with reddish-brown rust, and grabbed the oars, wordlessly paddling to the middle of Yule Lake, which was their favorite fishing spot. The water was still and calm, and a heron glided noiselessly above them. The sky was a perfect watercolor of pale blue unmarred by a single cloud, and it was surprisingly mild for a midsummer afternoon. Kayla breathed in the sweet air and wondered, with a wave of pure contentment and happiness that she would recall later that night with sickened horror, if the day could possibly be any more perfect.

Mark cast his line, then smiled when Kayla passed her pole to him. "Seriously?"

She groaned. "You know I hate baiting hooks, Daddy."

"You've got to learn how to do it sooner or later."

"I know how. I just don't want to."

He shook his head, but his crooked smile remained as he took her pole and proceeded to impale a frantically wiggling worm onto her hook.

Less than five minutes later she had a bite, and she yanked a silvery trout onto the boat.

"Look at that!" Mark exclaimed as he examined the fish. "That's probably your biggest one yet!"

"Nah, I think the one from Hunter's Stream was bigger," Kayla said.

She carefully eased the hook out of the flailing fish's mouth and tossed it back. They didn't fish for keeps. They never did. It was the act of fishing itself, basking in the day and each other's company on the gently rocking boat, that they enjoyed.

"Did I ever tell you how you were named, Kayla?" Mark asked suddenly as he twitched his pole slightly to the left. The gentle breeze ruffled his almost-white hair.

She glanced up, startled. "No, you've never told me." This was another thing she loved about their fishing trips; her father always told her an interesting story.

Mark fumbled a pack of cigarettes out of his front shirt pocket with his free hand. He rarely smoked, but no Mark Hudson story was complete without a faint haze of cigarette smoke lingering around his head.

"I originally wanted to name you Judith, you know."

Against her will Kayla giggled. "Judith, really? I'm glad you changed your mind."

He grinned, and the cigarette bobbed in his mouth. "Your mother changed it for me." Sadness flickered across his eyes, which were beginning to show the faint, bleary first signs of cataracts. Again she marveled at just how much he seemed to have aged in just four years. "Judith was my great-grandmother's name, and she'd just passed away when Gloria found out she was pregnant. So I suggested her name for the baby, if it were to be a girl."

"Mom didn't like the name?"

"It wasn't that." He took a deep drag of the cigarette. "She just told me, 'There are better ways of honoring the dead than passing on a name. A name is just a name. Memories, though, are real. You can't replace memories. Remember the past, don't live for it.'"

Kayla watched ripples dance across the black water as a frog leaped from the shore and splashed into the lake. "That's pretty good advice."

"She was a remarkable woman," Mark said quietly as he stared at the water. "Every day she faced the world with a kind word and a smile. Nothing could keep her down for long. Some days the only thing that kept me going was knowing that, if life ever knocked me down, Gloria would be right beside me to pick me back up again."

"What kept you going after?" Kayla murmured as she stared at the lake without really seeing it.

"You," Mark said simply.

Kayla said nothing, but her heart ached. On days like today, she missed her mother more than ever.

Gloria Hudson had died in a car accident nine years ago. Kayla often thought that her mother had been the glue that held their tiny family together. Certainly she'd always seemed to be able to bridge the gap between Kayla and her father, and when she passed away, Kayla felt that fissure deepen every day.

"Anyway," Mark continued, "she never could decide on a name until we were in the hospital. Kayla Nelson was the name of the nurse who helped deliver you, I'll never forget that. Your mother decided right then and there that she was going to name you after that nurse."

Kayla raised her eyebrows. "Really?"

"Really," Mark said with a thin smile. "How's that for living in the present?"

"Sounds like Mom, all right."

They passed the next several minutes in a comfortable, thoughtful silence. Finally, Mark broke it.

"I've never been good with words, Kayla. But I just want you to know that I'm sorry. One of the reasons we clash so much is that we're simply too much alike. But when I look at you, I also see your mother looking right back at me, and it's painful."

Kayla took her father's hand in her own and squeezed it reassuringly. "I miss her too. But we still have each other."

Mark returned her smile. "Yeah. Yeah, that's right."

The rest of the afternoon passed by much too quickly for Kayla. She couldn't remember a time before her mother's death when she and her father had gotten along this well. They hadn't caught many fish, but she didn't care about that; what she did care about was her father's easy smile and musical laughter as they talked, rehashing and reliving old memories that were sweet rather than bitter.

As the sun began to dip lower in the horizon, Kayla and Mark wordlessly rowed the boat towards the shore.

"I'm so glad we did this, Daddy," Kayla said as they climbed out of the boat.

"Me too," Mark said with a slight grimace.

Her smile faltered a little. Mark had shown no signs of pain for a few hours, and she'd foolishly allowed herself to cautiously believe that he was feeling better. "Are you sure you're okay?"

"I'm fine." Little pain lines settled around his eyes as he reached down to grab his pole and tackle box from the boat's compartment.

She grabbed his arm and stopped him. "No. I'll get it. You're hurting, and you can't convince me otherwise."

He hesitated, then nodded. "All right." He took a step backward and allowed her to unload their gear.

Unease flickered in her heart. Mark had never backed down from physical labor in his life, and normally he'd be ashamed of the thought of allowing his daughter to carry his own load. She realized that he really must be in more pain than she'd thought.

Her joy and contentment vanished on the spot, and she only felt a burning, gnawing worry in the pit of her stomach.

"Come on," she said gently, struggling to hold onto the armful of fishing gear. "It's not far to the truck."

That was true, but their truck was parked at the end of Yule Road, which was at the top of a steep hill. As they ponderously made their way up the road, she stole glances at her father. His normally tanned skin had gone the color of spoiled milk, and beads of sweat gathered on his forehead like glistening jewels. His face was twisted in pain, and his chest heaved.

"Daddy?"

His knees buckled and he fell, collapsing on the uneven red dirt road.

With a cry, she dropped the fishing poles and rushed over to him. She rolled him over on his back.

Cold panic coursed through her veins. What should she do?

He gasped for breath, his once powerful chest heaving weakly. His hands shook as she grasped them.

"Daddy, what's wrong?" she cried. She was almost immobilized in her panic.

His eyes, cloudy and hazy with pain, found hers. His mouth began to work, as if he were trying to speak.

"Don't say anything," she pleaded. Her mind raced almost as quickly as her heart. Finally, she remembered—his cell phone. She'd left hers in the truck, but he'd brought his, stashed it in the tackle box in case of an emergency.

She tried to pull away from him, but his grip was like iron.

She gently tried to pry his fingers away, but he tightened his hold on her and pulled her closer to him.

"Daddy, let me go, I need to call an ambulance—"

"Listen to me," he wheezed. Fear and pain warred with the stark urgency shining in his eyes. "Talk to…" his voice trailed away as he struggled to take a breath.

"Don't try to talk, just take it easy—"

"Talk to Emerson. Lewiston…wolves. Wolves, Kayla, your mother…" His voice grew weak and faint, and his grip on her slackened. That above all else scared her the most, and she sprang to her feet and rushed to the tackle box.

"911, what's your—"

"My dad!" she screamed into the phone, cutting off the brisk female voice. She ran a shaking hand through her hair. "I think he's having a heart attack, he collapsed."

"Where are you?"

She took a deep breath; for a split second, her panic was so great that she couldn't remember where she was. "Yule Road, about halfway to the lake."

"Just keep calm, paramedics are on their way."

"What can I do for him?" Her voice came out in a weak, helpless whimper.

"At the moment, nothing. Just wait with him."

She hung up and tossed the phone to the side, rushing back to her father's prone figure. She gripped his hand, noting how cold and pale his skin was. His breathing was shallow, and his eyes were half-open.

"Daddy, hold on, you're going to be okay," she said through numb lips.

"Kayla…"

She could barely hear him, and leaned across his face.

"Love…"

His breath had been tickling her ear, and suddenly the sensation stopped. She sat up, her eyes wide, like a frightened animal's.

His chest rose one last time, then settled down slowly. It didn't rise again.

Chapter 4

The phone rang. It was as piercing and shrill as a woman's scream in the silent cabin, but Kayla barely heard it. She sat on the couch, her half-open, glassy eyes glued to the blank television screen. Her hands were folded primly in her lap.

She hadn't moved in over an hour.

Her hair was lank and unkempt; she hadn't showered since Mark's funeral the previous morning. Her mind was as blank as the TV, and that was good; if she wasn't thinking about anything, she wouldn't have to think about her father.

The phone finally stopped ringing; whoever was calling had given up, it seemed. She was glad. There was no possible way on earth she could summon up the energy to get up off the couch and answer it.

She found herself thinking about her father, and she tried as hard as she could to pull her thoughts away, to go back to her blissfully blank state, but the sound of the ringing phone seemed to have pierced through her mind like a needle, popping the numb bubble around her mind, and now all sorts of thoughts and emotions that she'd willed herself to bury deep within her came bubbling up to the surface.

Her lower lip trembled and tears gathered in her eyes before finally slipping down her pale cheeks.

Her father had been pronounced dead before they'd even reached the hospital. She'd been almost insane with grief, and she remembered with a pang the last time she saw his body—aside from the viewing, that is, but she didn't really count that; when he'd been laid out in the coffin, dressed in a suit and tie, he hadn't looked like himself at all—as the nurses wheeled him away, covered in a white sheet.

She remembered how the doctor had approached her. He'd been reduced to nothing but a blur, so thick and heavy with her tears, and pulled her aside. He'd inquired if she were the next of kin. She hadn't been able to speak, but she nodded.

The doctor had offered his condolences, which hadn't comforted Kayla in the slightest, and handed her a clipboard. While she filled out the paperwork, she had been able to clear her throat and ask the question that had haunted her ever since Mark had collapsed.

"My father…" her voice was thin and strangled, and she tried again. "My father. Was it a heart attack?"

"We won't know for certain until the autopsy is complete, but at the moment, yes, that's my diagnosis."

Kayla had shaken her head, sending tears flying. "I just can't believe this. I can't believe this is happening."

The doctor had raised his bushy eyebrows, but when he spoke, his voice was surprisingly gentle. "With all due respect, Ms. Hudson, I don't understand how this could have come as a surprise."

"What do you mean?" Her brain was sluggish and slow, and she was still reeling with shock and mental exhaustion.

The doctor had blinked. "I mean Mark's condition. I was the one who diagnosed him two years ago. I tried to talk him out of it, I really did. But in the end, it was his choice, and no matter how unfair it seems, we all just have to respect that."

"What in the hell are you talking about?" Kayla's eyebrows had drawn together as the first flickers of anger and disbelief began to break through the heavy clouds of grief in her heart.

The doctor had looked nervous. "I...he didn't tell you?"

She'd shaken her head, and the doctor looked unsure of himself before finally clearing his throat and saying, "Ms. Hudson, your father had stage three congestive heart failure."

Her mouth had dropped open, and she had been aware that she probably looked stupid, but she had never been further from caring in her life.

"His general condition has been deteriorating for years, and after his heart failed I warned him that, without treatment, his chances of having a heart attack would greatly increase."

"And you didn't do anything?" she accused. Her fists had clenched involuntarily and her fingernails had pierced her skin, but she'd barely registered the pain.

"He refused treatment. In the eyes of the law, there was nothing we could do. We have to respect the patient's choice in matters of life or death."

Her mind had been sent reeling. While this certainly explained her father's declining health, she had no idea why he would refuse medical treatment. He had a comfortable amount of money in his savings account, and since he was retired, he no longer had to worry about missing work.

And why didn't he tell her?

On top of everything else, it was the realization of this secret that he'd kept from her, this final, greatest secret—or so she thought at the time—that had sent her into the listless, apathetic state that she'd been in ever since.

She barely remembered the wake or the funeral, which had both passed in a blur. One thing that had stood out to her, because it seemed odd and she couldn't shake the feeling that she was missing something, was the sheer number of people that had attended his funeral. There had been almost two hundred people, a sizable chunk of the town population.

Mark had always been a loner. To her knowledge, he'd had a scant handful of close friends and a few work acquaintances. That was all. He'd always more or less kept to himself. So why had so many people shown up to his funeral?

She remembered how person after person had come up to her, taking her hand and mumbling their condolences. She supposed that most of them must have known Mark when he was younger, maybe high school acquaintances or something, because almost everyone in attendance had been Mark's age or older. She had been the youngest one there.

Now, she frowned a little. Her face hurt a bit at the gesture; it had been slack and expressionless for so long. Now, after recalling her father's funeral, a touch of disquiet had wormed its way into her mind. She couldn't shake the feeling that something wasn't right. She thought hard, thinking about what that might be, but kept coming up empty.

Hers eyes stung with tears. Her father was dead, dead just a few weeks after she'd finally reconciled with him, and just like that her face broke out of its mask.

Tears rolled down her cheeks, her chest heaved as she sobbed, and she drew her knees up to her chest as she laid down on the couch, which still smelled like her father's cologne, and cried. The sound of her crushing grief echoed through the empty cabin.

Finally, after what seemed like ages, her tears dried up. She took a watery breath and sat up, wiping the moisture from her face.

She felt a little better...not much, but a little. The tears she'd cried seemed cleaner, her grief purer. She still hurt, she still hurt a lot, but something in her chest seemed to loosen.

"At least he didn't die alone," she said quietly to herself. Her voice was choked and rusty from disuse, and the sound of it startled her a little. "And at least I came back. We made up. We had a little bit of time together."

Not enough time, it was true, but it was something. And she knew that she would have never forgiven herself if her father had died before they'd made up.

Her stomach rumbled, and she blinked in surprise. She was hungry, immensely hungry. Ravenous, in fact. She hadn't eaten since her father had died.

She drifted into the kitchen and opened the fridge. The sight of the six-pack of her father's favorite beer sitting in there sent a jolt of pain through her heart—Mark had put it there before the ill-fated fishing trip, and now he would never drink it. She forced herself not to look at it.

After she'd eaten, she gathered up her clothes and took a shower. The hot water was soothing as it pounded on her aching body, washing away some of the pain and stress.

She was beginning to live again—just one step at a time, true, but it was a relief to be up and moving around again.

She got dressed, considered blow-drying her hair, and then decided that maybe she wasn't feeling quite that energetic. She sat down on the couch and flipped through channels.

It felt good to be able to think clearly again. But this only brought more questions to the front of her mind, questions she hadn't even allowed herself to consider at this point.

What came next?

What would she do? She only came back to her tiny New York town to see her father. Now that he was gone, she was at a loss as to what she would do next. She thought if she had to live in this house alone much longer, in the cabin that reminded her of Mark everywhere she looked, she would go crazy—and yet she couldn't bring herself to leave the last bit of her father's legacy behind. Not yet. It was painful to stay here, but she couldn't imagine leaving.

A series of sharp raps at the door startled her out of her reverie.

She slowly walked towards the door and opened it. "Hello?" she said cautiously as she did. Then a slow smile, her first smile in days, stretched across her face.

"Uncle Emerson!" she cried, pleased.

Emerson returned her smile, but it looked strained. "Hey, girl," he said with a feeble stab at cheerfulness.

Elliot Emerson—he insisted on going by his surname, and often said that if any of his friends called him Elliot he would knock their teeth out—wasn't her real uncle, but he was as good as. He'd been her father's best friend for as long as she could remember. Mark had had a small group of close friends (his buddies, he'd always called them) but Emerson had been his closest, and Mark had often called him his brother.

She swung the door open, and at her invitation Emerson stepped inside. He was a huge African American man with broad shoulders and thick, muscular forearms.

She vaguely remembered seeing him at Mark's funeral. He'd given a grave, solemn speech, and had spoken to Kayla briefly after it was all over. But she'd been half out of her mind, and could hardly remember what he had said to her.

He took off his dirty orange cap, the one he always wore, and wrung it in his hands. His expression was strange—simultaneously sorrowful and nervous.

"Kayla," his said in his deep, slow voice. "I'm so, so sorry. God knows I can never say anything to ease your pain, but I'm sorry that this happened."

She bit her lower lip to keep it from trembling, and her sight doubled and wavered as tears sprung to her eyes again. Emerson's words touched her in a way that the condolences of the doctor and all the strangers at the funeral never could. With a jolt, she realized that Emerson was probably the one person on earth who had known her father better than she had. Certainly they had known each other longer.

"I'm sorry too," she said quietly. "Are you…are you doing okay?"

Emerson hesitated. "I've been better. That man was my brother, I don't care what our birth certificates say."

"I know." Kayla dabbed at her face with her sleeve and wondered when she would ever stop crying.

"What about you? You're looking a little better since the funeral. You didn't look…well, you didn't look quite all there, if you forgive me for saying so."

"I wasn't, not really." She brushed a lock of her long, wet hair away from her face. "I'm a little better now. Well, I'm thinking more clearly, at least."

When Emerson spoke, his voice was incredibly gentle. "Mark was a great man, and he always loved you. Even after…you know…"

She nodded stiffly. "Even after I ran out on him. Yeah."

"That wasn't your fault. Mark always blamed himself, you know."

"I didn't want him to blame himself," she said fiercely. "It was my fault. It was."

"It was both of your faults. The Hudsons are too stubborn for their own good, I've always said that."

She let out a watery chuckle and turned towards the kitchen. "Do you want anything to drink?" she called out behind her. "There's some Black Label in here that my dad put away." Her heart lurched, but she ignored it. "I don't drink beer, and it would be a shame to let it all go to waste."

"Not today, but thank you."

He sounded strange, and she turned back towards him. He was wringing the cap between his hands so fast she was afraid he was going to rip it, and his eyes were darting around the room like a trapped animal's. She'd never seen Emerson look this nervous; he was usually cool, calm, and collected.

"Emerson, what's going on?"

He swallowed, tried to smile weakly, and failed. He let out a sigh. "Kayla, did your father say anything before he died?"

Her eyebrows slanted together in a frown. She'd purposely avoided thinking about her father's death, about that awful moment when he'd collapsed to the ground like an ancient, rotting tree, and the expression of stark fear, peeking through the pain in his face, as he realized that he was dying. That was possibly the worst part. It was just too painful; she never wanted to relive that moment as long as she lived.

She turned her eyes up towards Emerson, her heart leaping in her chest. "Yeah. Yeah, I forgot about it until just now."

"What did he say?" The urgency in Emerson's voice was impossible to miss.

"He said your name. Something about my mother. And wolves. He said 'wolves' a lot, but I don't know what he meant."

"Nothing else?"

Kayla felt a strong flash of mingled irritation and disquiet. "I don't know. Uncle Emerson, what's wrong?"

He glanced around the room, swallowed, and finally sighed. "I held out as long as I could. I really did. I didn't want to drop this on you out of nowhere, not after your father just passed, but I can't wait any longer."

"What?" Unease flickered in her chest.

"The rest of the guys wanted to come, to talk to you, but I told them to leave you to me. I thought you might believe me. I mean, I've known you since you were about yay-high." He lowered his hand to his knee. "I've watched you grow from a headstrong, tomboyish toddler to a scared little girl who'd lost her mother to the beautiful young lady you are today. Now you need to listen to what I'm saying, okay?"

She nodded.

"Do you trust me?"

She didn't even have to think; she nodded again.

"Okay." He paced around the room for a moment, seemed to come to a decision, and faced her again. "Kayla, your father was a werewolf."

Chapter 5

Kayla stared at the man who had served as her uncle as long as she could remember. His eyes were wide and pleading, and his entire body was tense. He looked as serious as death itself.

She threw her head back and laughed.

She laughed until her stomach ached and tears—what a relief from the painful, mournful tears she'd cried for days—ran down her cheeks. She laughed because what he'd said was ridiculous, and she laughed to keep herself from entertaining the idea that he was telling the truth.

A muscle twitched in Emerson's jaw, but otherwise he showed no signs of resentment at being laughed at. "Kayla—"

"No," she giggled, but her amusement had vanished. She crossed her arms and tried to keep a straight face. "No, that's ridiculous."

"I'm telling you the truth," he said in a slow, measured voice.

Kayla narrowed her eyes. "Just stop it." She turned away from him and gazed out of the kitchen window. The sun was just beginning to set, casting the edge of the forest in a cozy golden glow. "I'm surprised at you, Uncle Emerson. I never had you pegged as the type of person to make jokes about my dead father." She injected her voice with as much venom as possible. She realized that she was angry, angry at her uncle for trying to trick her into thinking that he was serious.

She whirled back around. "Why would you even say that?"

"Because it's the truth," he said patiently, then rushed to explain, as if he was afraid that she'd interrupt him again. "Listen, don't you remember anything strange about your father?"

"No," she said sharply, but she was afraid that her doubt showed on her face. The fact was she'd been suspicious about Mark's behavior for a while now.

"Really?" he asked skeptically. "You haven't noticed anything odd at all? You didn't think it was strange that he disappeared for half a day or more at a time? Or that he forbade you from visiting Lewiston? Yes, he told me about that," he said, raising a hand to cut off Kayla's question. "He didn't seem afraid for you?"

"It wasn't my business where he was going or why he didn't want me around Lewiston," she said shortly. "And if he was afraid for me…well, lots of fathers are protective of their daughters."

"All right, Kayla," he said as he rubbed his temples, as if he were getting a headache. "What about your mother, then?"

"What about her?"

"Do you really believe that her death was an accident?"

Something squeezed Kayla's heart. Her lips thinned and she glared at Emerson. "Of course it was, and you leave my mother out of this." She was trembling now. "That's enough. Werewolves aren't real!" Her voice rose in pitch, and she realized that she was shouting. She took a deep breath, and when she spoke her voice was calmer, more normal-sounding. "Werewolves aren't real," she repeated.

But Emerson looked more thoughtful than anything else. "Yes, I suppose you're right. Werewolves, in the sense that most people know them, aren't real. The whole full-moon thing, silver bullets, half-man half-wolf? Yeah, that's crap. I guess what you'd really call us are shapeshifters."

Kayla's brain was whirling in disbelief. She shook her head. "I'm sorry, what? Us? You think you're a werewolf, too?"

"I know I am. I was born one. So was your father."

"Get out," she said suddenly. Her anger bubbled to the surface, as hot and strong as molten lava, and she was done. Done listening to lies, done entertaining ridiculous notions. Her fists clenched. "I love you like you're my own kin, Emerson, but I've had enough. My father is dead, and I need to grieve. You're more than welcome to come back when you're through spouting nonsense."

He sighed, his shoulders slumping in resignation. "I was hoping that it wouldn't come to this. I really was. But like I said, the Hudsons are too stubborn for their own good. There's only one way to make you see the truth."

"What on earth are you talking about now?" she asked wearily.

"Please don't be too frightened. This will come as a shock to you, but I'm still your uncle and I promise I won't hurt you."

"What—"

She let out a gasp, then a frightened whimper as Emerson's outline shimmered. A bright, blinding light flashed through the room, and Kayla stumbled, pressing her back against the kitchen counter and grasping it with both hands to stop from trembling. Her eyes grew wider and wider in her face, and she could feel her face drain of color. She felt simultaneously hot and cold as terror and shock shot through her.

She heard the minute sound of ripping fabric and something heavy thumping on the hardwood floor.

Her eyes watered, but she couldn't look away from the bright light.

Then it faded, and Kayla let out an involuntary whimper.

In her uncle's place stood an enormous, shaggy wolf.

Its fur was as black as a moonless night sky. It was huge, reaching nearly to her abdomen. Its eyes were a bright golden color, and in them shone an unmistakable intelligence. It opened its mouth and panted, revealing sharp, white teeth.

It took a step toward her, and instinct took over; Kayla turned her back and fled, fled away from the wolf that by all rights shouldn't have been there, and dashed to the nearest door, which led to the bathroom.

She slammed the door shut and pressed her back against it as she sank to the floor. Her entire body trembled, and she forced herself to take a deep breath. She closed her eyes.

She was losing her mind. That was the only explanation. She had finally cracked under the strain, and the grief of losing her father was causing her to hallucinate. There was nothing else that could explain what she had just seen.

She took deep, measured breaths, but her heart still raced. Her stomach churned, and she was deeply afraid that she might puke.

She could hear the wolf's claws clicking on the floor as it approached the closed door. She gulped. Then, without missing a beat, the sound of the paws turned to the sound of footsteps thumping across the floor.

Sharp, rapid knocks vibrated the door, and Kayla instinctively flinched away and slowly rose to her feet, gripping the sink to keep from collapsing.

"Kayla," Emerson called softly through the door.

"Go away!" she cried. She could hear the panic, which was really more like borderline hysteria, in her voice.

"Kayla, listen to me," he said urgently. "That was the only way you'd ever believe me."

"I'm going insane," she murmured. "You're not there, nobody's there. Any moment now I'm going to wake up in a mental hospital."

"You're not crazy, I promise." His voice was soft, gentle, and disarming, and to her surprise she found that it had a calming effect on her; the tremors racking her body slowly eased, although she was still terrified. "I'm real. You're not imagining things."

"But it's just not possible," she whispered through numb lips.

"It is. Open up, and I'll explain what I can."

The genuine concern in his voice pierced through her confusion and terror, and against every instinct screaming in her mind, she slowly approached the door and swung it open. She flinched, half-expecting to see a huge, snarling wolf, but it was only Emerson—Emerson, whom she loved and trusted.

He was wearing one of her father's holey T-shirts and a pair of his sweatpants; she assumed he must have fetched some spare clothes from her father's bedroom before transforming back into himself. She swallowed, painfully aware of how ridiculous and impossible that sounded in her mind.

"Come with me," Emerson said gently, and without any conscious thought she followed him back into the kitchen.

He turned his back toward her, and she heard the soft clinking of mugs.

He turned back around and set a huge mug of fragrant tea in front of her. He pulled a bottle of brandy out of Mark's liquor cabinet and poured a carefully measured dollop into it. He stirred the tea and handed the mug to her. "Drink this. You'll feel better. You're probably in shock, and I take full responsibility for that, but I had no other choice. You had to see."

She took a huge gulp of the tea, grimaced, and took another gulp. "Why?" she asked finally. She glanced up at Emerson, her eyes wide. "If this is real, why?

Why couldn't you just let me go on believing what I believed?"

"First things first," Emerson said quietly. He stood up, walked away, rummaged in the debris of his torn clothes, and when he came back he was holding a slim black notebook in his hands.

"What's this?" Kayla asked blankly as he handed it to her. The brandy was doing wonders; her limbs stopped trembling and her heart had resumed something like its normal pace.

"Your father came to me a couple of days after you'd come home from college. He looked rather distraught, and was holding this book in his hands. He gave it to me and told me that, in the event of his death, I should deliver it to you. In it, he explains everything."

Kayla's brain was fuzzy; from grief, exhaustion, shock, and now the brandy. "In the event of his death…Uncle Emerson, did you know about his condition?"

"I did."

"And you didn't tell me?" she cried angrily.

"He told me not to," Emerson said simply. "In the end, I had to trust that he knew what was best for you."

She was breathing heavily through her nose, but against her will she slowly nodded. "Yeah, that sounds like my dad all right."

Emerson nodded towards the notebook and stood up. "Read it. By the time that you're done, I should be back."

"Where are you going?"

"To go get the rest of the guys. They need to speak with you."

"The guys?"

"Your father's friends." He paused. "Well, no. His pack. His brothers. Your father was the leader, the alpha wolf, of the Youngstown wolf pack."

"Pack," she murmured as a chill ran down her spine. The word sounded strange and foreign in her throat.

As Emerson left, Kayla turned the notebook over and over in her hands. She didn't want to read it. She still thought she might be losing her mind, but in the event that she wasn't?

She didn't want to learn any more unpleasant secrets about her father. She wanted him to remain in her memory as he was—gruff, stubborn, independent, and vulnerable in ways that perhaps only she knew. And human.

But in the end, the pull of her own curiosity and her desire to know the truth was too great to ignore.

Between Two Packs

She opened the notebook and flipped to the first page.

Chapter 6

My dearest Kayla,

If you're reading this, then that means I am no longer on this earth.

I'm sorry that I never told you about my diagnosis. For the first time in four years, I had you back. I couldn't bear to destroy your happiness.

Also, and this is a little closer to the truth, I didn't know how. Every time I decided that you deserved to know, that I was being selfish by keeping you in the dark, I couldn't bring myself to do it. The words always got stuck in my throat, and I would look at you, see how much you looked like your mother, and think, well, maybe it's for the best.

Words can never describe how much I love you, Kayla, and how proud I am of the beautiful, intelligent woman you've become.

After I lost your mother, I pushed you away. I was grieving, and I guess a part of me didn't want to see that you were grieving, too. I can never make up for that. All I can say is that I'm sorry.

"I'm sorry too, Daddy," she whispered as tears slipped down her cheeks. She wiped them away and kept reading.

Now, to the part I'm sure you're full of questions about.

I told Emerson that it was important that you believe that he was telling the truth before you read this journal. I don't know if he convinced you, or if he showed you (that seems more like Emerson, to be honest; he's always been the type to just cut to the chase). But either way, you know, and that's what matters.

It's true, Kayla. I am a werewolf, a shapeshifter.

I've been one for as long as I can remember. I first turned when I was five years old. My father, your grandpa, was one too, and he was the alpha of the Youngstown pack in his younger days. He taught me everything that I know today.

There's still much that I don't understand, but I've been able to fill in the blanks, thanks in part to testimonies I've heard from other shifters and my own common sense.

The shifter gene is genetic, passed from father to son. I've met no female shifters in my time, and I can assume that the gene is only present in males. I'm sure that you were probably wondering, in the back of your mind, if you were a shapeshifter, too. Well, you're not, Kayla. You're safe, don't worry.

She paused. Part of her, the part of her that was slowly warming up to the idea that this was real, not a prank or a hallucination, *had* been wondering that. She took a deep breath and kept reading.

Werewolves are only one type of shifter. There are others, I've met some—people that can turn into bears, panthers, tigers, lions, owls, and many others. I even met a cow shifter once— one day you'll have to get Emerson to tell you that story, it's hilarious.

Very few people know about shifters. Up until about a hundred years or so ago, they were more or less accepted as real. In fact, many shifters lived side by side along the more tolerant humans.

Right before the First World War, before my grandfather was born, a strong group of shapeshifter hunters who called themselves the Bane rose up and traveled the country, slaughtering all known shifters and their families. Thousands of innocent people died, and the shapeshifter gene was in danger of disappearing altogether.

We were on the verge of extinction, Kayla. My great-grandfather knew that something had to be done, or all shifters would die out. So he gathered all who remained in America, a hundred or so shifters, and retaliated against the Bane.

It was a long, bitter, drawn-out war. Almost nobody knew that as American citizens fought and died on foreign soil another, smaller war was being waged right underneath their noses.

It took three years, but the shifters succeeded. The Bane was eradicated, and finally shifters could live in peace.

The war took its toll, however. Shifters are rare in this country, though from what I can understand they're thriving in remote, less developed parts of the world, like Zimbabwe and Brazil.

All this might sound irrelevant, but I think it's important for you to know your history; all of it.

I met your mother when we were both very young. I was eighteen, and at that point I was second-in-command of the pack. I was a reckless, fearless, wayward young man, and she was smart and quiet and kind. She grounded me and gave me a reason to look forward.

She accidentally found out about me—the real me—while we were taking a romantic getaway camping trip in the lower Catskills. A bear charged at us out of nowhere, and seeing the danger she was in I didn't even think; I transformed and chased the bear away.

She had a much easier time accepting it than I imagine you are at the moment. After we got back to the cabin and I explained everything to her, I realized just how extraordinary she was, and how I was already head over heels in love with her. So I proposed to her right then and there. I built the cabin, we got married, I took over the pack as alpha after my father passed away, and not long afterwards you were born.

I was glad you were a girl and therefore wouldn't inherit the gene. I was always damn proud to be a shapeshifter—I still am—but I wanted you to be free of the burden that comes along with the gift. Hence the reason why I never told you about me.

I wanted you to live a normal life. It was too late for your mother, but not for you. She disapproved. She always thought you should know the truth, but she went along with it.

But then…

God, Kayla, you'll never know how hard it is to write this. I can only imagine how overwhelmed you must feel right now, with me revealing secret after secret…just please believe that I lied to you because I love you and I wanted to keep you safe.

I always told you your mother had died in a car accident. But the truth is, she was murdered.

Coldness enveloped her, and all the moisture evaporated from her mouth.

She was attacked and killed by another wolf shifter on the outskirts of Lewiston. She was only going to get groceries, but her car was found abandoned and her body was discovered in the woods, mangled. I don't know what she was doing in the forest; I can only assume that the man responsible lured her out of her car and into the woods.

I lost my mind that night. Do you remember how I left you with Emerson for two days after the funeral? I shouldn't have done that, I should have stayed there with you. Add it to my list of regrets.

I spent those two days hunting down the son of a bitch responsible. I killed him.

More than anything she wanted to toss the book aside and run, just get up and run somewhere, run away from the awful words she was reading, but she couldn't. Her father, the man she'd loved even in the moments when she hated him, was both a werewolf and a murderer.

She forced herself to keep reading even as her stomach churned.

It gets worse, believe it or not.

I wasn't satisfied. I was convinced that he had outside help, that he was connected with someone. I've spent all the years since searching for evidence, and finally, three years ago while you were away in college, I discovered something. The man who killed your mother was a member of another pack of werewolves.

You were gone, and I had nothing to lose. I swore vengeance, and with Emerson at my side I declared war on the other pack.

We are at a disadvantage. We're all old, and none of us are passing on our genes. The other pack is stronger, younger, and more arrogant.

This pack lives and operates in Lewiston.

Now do you understand why I never wanted you over there? Those sons of bitches would stop at nothing to win this war, and that includes hurting you to get to me.

After a while, I could no longer ignore my failing health, and I went to the doctor. When he told me what was wrong and that I potentially had little time left, I refused treatment. I still had much to do, and I couldn't waste precious time in a hospital.

I expected the war to be over by now. I really did.

The last thing I want is for you to be involved, Kayla. Believe me, it's the very last thing. But at this point I have no choice.

Emerson will explain the rest; it's late, and I'm tired. I can barely catch my breath.

Please believe me when I say I only ever had the best of intentions for you. I wouldn't blame you if you resented me or even hated me for the secrets I kept from you. I'm still just a man, and I've made more than my fair share of mistakes, especially in areas that concerned you. I'm not a great father, I admit that. But I love you. I always have, and I always will.

She flipped through the rest of the book, but it was blank.

She set it down on the table. She felt oddly calm and…well, peaceful. The feeling was so foreign to her that she had to puzzle it out for a moment to understand what she was feeling.

"I love you too, Daddy," she said quietly.

She closed her eyes, took a deep breath, and finally allowed herself to fully and completely accept the truth.

Chapter 7

"Are you all right, Kayla?" Emerson asked as he anxiously scanned her face.

"I'm fine," she replied, and although it wasn't exactly the truth, it didn't feel like a lie, either. Her entire viewpoint had been shaken and she'd been ruthlessly forced to look at the world, and especially her still-painful memories of her father, in an entirely new light.

"We're all sorry that you had to be pulled into this," John Healy said in his slow, mournful voice. That voice, coupled with his long ears and his droopy, bloodshot eyes, reminded Kayla of an old bloodhound. She had to clamp her teeth together to keep in a giggle. God, she was losing it. She felt like both laughing and weeping at the same time, so great was her shock and weariness.

There was a certain calm in accepting the truth, however. The more she thought about it, the more things that clicked into place—things about her father and vague, half-forgotten childhood memories came flooding to the forefront of her mind, all crowding together and vying for attention.

She shook her head and tried to focus on the men in front of her.

True to his word, Emerson had returned with the rest of her father's friends...his pack, she corrected herself in her mind. There were six men, including Emerson, and she was familiar with all of them, if not as close to them as she was to her father's best friend. They had all been more or less constant figures in her childhood. Not a one of them was under the age of fifty-five at the very least, and Paulie Karson was the oldest at eighty-three; he was nearly blind and blinked feebly up at the strong kitchen lights as if he hadn't the faintest clue where he was.

Jesus, Kayla thought with wonder. *These men are fighting a war? They look as if they can't even walk up a flight of stairs without some difficulty. What on earth was my father thinking?*

She looked around at the men—John, Paulie, Harold, Larry, Mike, and Emerson—and saw that they were all looking at her expectantly, as if waiting for her to say something. She didn't know what to say—she had so many questions she wasn't sure how to start.

She cleared her throat. "I can't help but feel as if there's something I'm missing. Why come to me now? In my father's journal he also mentioned that he would need me for something after he died. What do I need to do?"

Emerson exchanged a look with the other men. "I wish I could give you more time to mourn your father. You need to heal and you need the time and the space to move on. But at the moment that's not possible. Please forgive us, Kayla." The rest of the old men nodded in agreement. "Your father was always a hot-tempered man. While I might not necessarily agree with his methods, he was my best friend, and most importantly, my alpha. I wholeheartedly support his decision to fight the Lewiston pack. They took from him, and you, something that could never in this world ever be replaced.

"Do I think that he should have taken a more diplomatic approach? Yes, I do, and I've told him so many times. But that doesn't change a thing. We're still at war."

"Get on with it, Emerson," Larry, a skinny man with white hair, interjected. "She's getting bored."

"No, I'm not," Kayla said honestly. Her eyes were glazed and her face was pale from exhaustion, but she was holding on to Emerson's every word.

Emerson took a sip of Kayla's second cup of brandy-spiked tea and continued. "I suppose I have to explain our laws and traditions a bit for you to really understand the gravity of the situation, Kayla." He sighed and glanced down at the table before finally meeting her eyes again. "Under normal circumstances, in the event of an alpha's death, his second-in-command, usually his son if he has one, will take over as alpha. An alpha can also step down if he wishes and pass the title on to the next highest-ranking man."

Kayla nodded. It all sounded pretty straightforward to her.

"However, if the pack has officially declared war, if the alpha dies, only a direct descendant, even if they do not possess the shapeshifter gene, can take control of the pack. It's an ancient tradition that, over time, has become more or less an ironclad law. It was implemented long ago to stop wartime power struggles within a pack. You can understand, I'm sure—people turning on each other's packmates in order to gain the title and the honor of leading the pack to victory in the war."

Kayla gaped at him. Surely he wasn't saying what she thought he was saying...

"We can't lose this war," Harold, a balding man who, in his mid-fifties, was the youngest man sitting at the table, said grimly.

"Why not?" she asked through numb lips. "Why can't you just...you know...call it quits?"

They all stared at her, and she shifted uncomfortably under their piercing gaze.

"Do you not want the men responsible for your mother's death brought to justice?" Larry asked incredulously.

"Of course I do," she replied with a snap of anger in her voice. "But...I mean, look at you!" She swept her hand around the table. "Not one of you is in good health, if you don't mind me saying so. He can barely even see!" She pointed at Paulie, who didn't respond; she rather thought that he couldn't hear her. "You're in absolutely no condition to fight!"

"It's out of the question, Kayla," Emerson said quietly.

"Why?!"

They all exchanged looks, and she couldn't help but notice their grave expressions. Finally, Mike answered her.

"Because according to werewolf law, the alpha or the alpha's closest living descendant as well as the second-in-command of the defeated pack will be executed and the remaining pack members will be exiled from the area. Sometimes the alpha's descendant can be spared, at the discretion of the victorious pack's alpha, but not often. Certainly we can't expect the other pack to show mercy."

"You and me, Kayla," Emerson said, sorrow flickering in his eyes. "If we don't win this war, we will die." Desperation filled his face. "Do you see now? Do you see why we have to win?"

She swallowed. Her throat was as dry as sandpaper.

Execution. Torn apart by wolves. Terror squeezed her heart, and for the first time since her father's death, doubt and just the tiniest hint of anger filled her mind.

He couldn't have left well enough alone? Now, thanks to him, seven of the people that he'd loved the most were facing exile or death.

"We'll probably die anyway," she pointed out. A cold trickle of dread ran down her spine.

"Maybe so, but at least we'll die fighting," John said firmly. But Kayla's panic only rose a notch.

What on earth was she going to do? She couldn't lead the pack!

"I don't know anything about war," she said, her voice shaking. "I don't even play *Call of Duty*, for God's sake! How am I supposed to lead you guys to victory when I didn't even know werewolves existed until an hour ago?" She was working herself into a frenzy of terror until Emerson placed his warm hand on top of her own.

"Relax, Kayla. You don't have to do anything, not really. I'll handle everything; you just have to assume the mantle of power, otherwise we'd have to forfeit the war and we'd lose everything regardless.

She breathed heavily through her nose. "I don't have to do anything?"

"No. Just accept the title. As of right now, you're an honorary werewolf. How does it feel?"

She uttered a shaky laugh. "Lousy. I wish I could go back to being ignorant."

"You'll get used to it," Emerson said dryly. He rubbed his hands together and offered her a strained smile. "All right, it's official. You're our leader, if only technically. Now we can proceed."

Kayla glanced around the table. She observed the men's stony faces and determined eyes, and she let out a shuddery sigh of defeat.

What on earth had her father gotten her into?

"So what's the plan?" she asked, trying to sound confident and bold as opposed to shaky and terrified.

Even confused old Paulie seemed to pay attention as Emerson leaned forward and said, "We need to go on the offensive."

Stunned silence greeted his words.

"For too long we've played the long game; setting up perimeters around their territory and dogging any stragglers who strayed over the border. That ends now. By now I'm sure they've heard of our leader's death, and I don't think they're expecting an attack any time soon. They're expecting us to take time to lick our wounds and mourn our alpha." He smacked the table, causing a sound like a shotgun blast that caused Kayla to jump. "That's exactly why we need to strike now!"

The men were murmuring their assent, their eyes gleaming, but a question gnawed at Kayla's mind.

"How many men...I mean, werewolves," she said slowly, still trying to get used to the idea, "are in the Lewiston pack?"

Emerson looked pained, and he took a moment to answer. "We're not sure. Maybe thirty."

Kayla drew in a hiss of breath.

"Yes, it's bad," Emerson said almost angrily. "Don't you think we know what we're up against?"

Thirty. Kayla glanced around the table; from Paulie, who was now humming quietly to himself; to John, with his droopy, sleepy face; and to Mike, who was rubbing the gnarled joints in his hands and wincing.

"They're going to tear you apart!" she declared. Tears stung her eyes.

She turned to Emerson—Emerson, who now had the most control over the pack. "You have to call it off," she begged. "You call it off or I will. We can run away." She addressed all of the men, pleading with her eyes. "Nobody has to die. My mother's death was avenged a long time ago. Nobody else has to get hurt over a stupid war!"

Emerson's eyes bored into hers. He was looking at her like he'd never looked at her before…with disgust. "You'd turn your back on your father's wishes like that?" he asked softly. "Your mother? Your home? Your *legacy,* for God's sake?"

"I just don't want anyone else to die," she whispered miserably.

"I can respect that," Emerson said in a slow, measured voice, as if he were trying not to lose his temper. "But as I've said, we have no choice. This is our best chance for survival." He turned to the rest of the group. "The word around Lewiston is that Harper is leaving town to visit a friend. He'll be leaving north on Highway 86 sometime tonight. Now we don't know exactly when, but we'll be ready when it gets dark. We'll wait all night if we have to. He'll never make it past the river. We'll lie in wait. If he's traveling in wolf form, all the easier for us. If he's traveling by car, we'll have to get him to stop somehow. Either way, this ends tonight. If we take him out, they'll be weak. William Burkhart will have to lead the pack, and under his command they'll crumble in a heartbeat. Burkhart is erratic and hot-tempered; he'll never be able to lead a large pack like Harper can."

The old men murmured agreement, but Kayla was lost. "Who's Harper?"

Emerson glanced at her. "The alpha wolf of the Lewiston pack. Adam Harper. A crafty son of a bitch who…what?"

For at that moment Kayla's jaw had dropped and her eyes widened. "I'm sorry, did you say his name is Adam?" She couldn't believe that the incredibly handsome and intimidating man that she'd seen was a werewolf, and one that, according to her father, was responsible for her mother's death.

Of course, she could be mistaken; Adam was a common name, after all, but in her heart she believed that she'd guessed right.

"Yes." Emerson stared at her. "Why?"

"Is he tall, with dark hair and a tribal tattoo on his shoulder?"

Now it was Emerson's turn to look surprised. "Yeah. Do you know him?"

"Just in passing." And she told them about her encounter with Adam at the donut shop.

John shook his head. The rest of the men, even Emerson, seemed momentarily speechless. "And he didn't attack you?"

"No, just gave me a dirty look."

"I'm shocked, honestly," Mike spoke up. "He's bound to know who you are and what you look like; he's a fool if he didn't do any research on the enemy.

I know we did. Anyway, I'm almost positive he looked at you that way because he *did* know who you are…I'm just surprised he didn't kill you to get to Mark. It's what I would have done."

"Did Mark know?" Emerson interjected.

Kayla nodded, biting her lip. "Yeah. We got into a fight about it. He seemed super paranoid." She glanced down at her hands, which were neatly folded on the shiny tabletop. "Now I understand why."

"I'm surprised he never told us. I suppose he didn't want to worry us," Emerson said.

Kayla lapsed into silence and listened to the men discuss their plan to ambush Adam that night. Unease gnawed at her heart. It didn't seem very fair. Then again, thirty against six wasn't fair at all, either.

She didn't want a war. She didn't want any more bloodshed, not after just having her father ripped from her life.

Regardless of what Emerson had said, Kayla knew that there had to be a way to avoid a fight. There just had to be.

As the men's voices faded away to a comfortable drone, a plan began to form in her mind. It wasn't a very smart plan, she knew that, but she was determined to form a truce between the two packs.

She'd do it. She had just enough of her father in her to believe that, with a hard enough head and just a dash of ingenuity, anything was possible.

Chapter 8

She glanced over her shoulder for what seemed like the tenth time and let out her breath in a shaky sigh of relief. She wasn't being followed. Good.

Ten minutes ago she'd murmured some excuse to the rest of the pack about needing to run to town for something and had then snuck out to her car. She hadn't been able to come up with anything better than that, but to her relief they hadn't questioned her; in fact, they had barely heard her, they had been so engrossed in their plans for tonight's strike.

If her plan worked, it would never happen.

She just couldn't believe that the two packs could hate each other so much that they'd be willing to kill the other off. Her own feelings were mixed up in the matter, too—grief for her father, disbelief and sorrow and anger over learning the truth of her mother's death, and above all else an overwhelming desire to have all of this over so that she could move on with her life.

She was now entering Lewiston; the thick coniferous trees were thinning, giving way to buildings and sidewalks and bright, blooming flowers.

As she idled at an intersection, she frowned.

She had no idea where to begin looking for the pack.

More specifically, she was looking for Adam. As alpha, he would be the one to talk to…and the more she thought about it, the more she was convinced that he would listen to her. He couldn't be that unreasonable; otherwise he might have attacked her that day in Lewiston. He easily could have followed her to her father's house and disposed of both the alpha and his daughter in one fell swoop. So why hadn't he?

The only answer she could think of was this: Adam didn't want this war, either.

She drummed her fingers nervously on the steering wheel. She was looking over her shoulder so frequently now that a painful crick had developed in her neck.

She was more than nervous; she was scared. She felt as if a large red target had been painted on her back, and here she was wandering into enemy territory.

But she had to trust that she could work this out. Nobody else had to get hurt.

But still the question remained. Where to look?

She drove around town aimlessly for half an hour, keeping an eye out for Adam's black Jaguar; it was so conspicuous that she'd have to be blind to miss it. But after she drove down each street twice, she finally had to admit to herself that her plan wasn't working.

Think, she ordered herself as she cruised into an empty parking space and shut off the engine. She closed her eyes and laid her head on the steering wheel. She was beginning to get a migraine.

She glanced at the dashboard clock. Her heart sank. It was nearly four. Nighttime in upstate New York came rather late in the summer, but she guessed that she only had a few hours before dark. She had to get to Adam before her father's pack did.

She bit her lip and tried to ignore her confusion. If her father was telling the truth, then Adam's pack was responsible for her mother's death. Did she really want to save the life of the man who, if only by association, killed her mother?

She let out a deep, shuddery sigh. Yes. Yes, she did. If Gloria had still been alive, she would have been appalled at her husband's behavior. She had to honor her mother, even if it meant she would deny her father.

She brought her attention back to the task at hand and tried to think. Finally, she thought of something.

Mark had built his cabin away from town, in the seclusion of the forest. His pack was really too small to have a need for a base, but for a large pack like Adam's? They would need a place to congregate, to meet up and discuss tactics, assuming that they didn't live together. And considering the history of all shapeshifters, they would probably harbor at least a little bit of mistrust towards humans. Also, they would probably feel the need for seclusion and pick a place that would be far away from prying human eyes. If she were a shifter, she was sure that she'd want to keep it a secret.

She smiled a little, proud of her detective work. It wasn't much to go on, but it was something. She would need to look for a dwelling that would be large enough to contain thirty or more people, a dwelling that would be far away from town.

She had no time to lose. She touched her keys, thinking of maybe asking a local where such a place might be, but before she could start the car, a rapping sound jerked her out of her thoughts. She whipped her head up.

Three men stood outside her car window. One of them grinned and lowered his hand; he'd knocked on the glass.

Fear shot through her heart. She glanced around. She'd pulled into the parking lot of a derelict, abandoned gas station. There were no other cars around, and the nearest building was nearly a block away.

She was alone.

The man who had tapped on the window grinned again. It was a frightening grin that exposed crooked yellow teeth that looked more like fangs. But his smile didn't touch his eyes, which were blank and expressionless. His hair, which was a shade of blond so fair that it was almost white, hung in his eyes.

He made a motion with his hand as if he wanted her to roll down her window. The other two men leaned casually against her car. One murmured something to the other, who then laughed.

Her veins felt as if a gallon of ice water had been dumped into her bloodstream. There was no way in hell she was going to roll down her window and talk to these men.

"Hey!" the blond man called through the glass. His voice was rough and gravelly. "Roll down your window, babe! We need to talk."

She heard the faint sound of the other two men giggling. Kayla's heart raced and she shook her head.

"Come on," the blond man said impatiently. "Don't make this any harder than it has to be."

He reached for her door handle, and Kayla didn't even pause to think; she cranked up her car and whipped out of the parking space, her hands clenched on the steering wheel so hard that her knuckles whitened. Her face was drained of color and a strangled little whimper forced its way through her numb lips. Her tires screeched on the pavement as she peeled down the street.

She whipped her head around. The men, who were standing on the edge of the street and shouting at her, gradually grew smaller and smaller as she fled.

Her plan had failed. There was no way she could go back to Lewiston now; Adam was on his own. She had to face the fact that there was no way she could stop the war. All she could do now was hope that her father's pack would somehow be able to win.

Tears of mingled terror and relief slipped down her cheeks. She was safe. She didn't know who the men were or what they wanted, but she wanted to be as far away from them as possible.

She was about half a mile away from the parking lot now and was nearing the town limit; she didn't see a single house, only the road stretching through the deep, thick forest. Although she was sure that she was far enough away from the three men to be reasonably safe, she couldn't resist the urge to look back over her shoulder one last time.

It was possibly one of the biggest mistakes of her life.

Everything happened so quickly that later, looking back, she could hardly remember what had happened. One moment everything was fine; the next, the metallic shrieking of crunching metal shattered the semi-silence and she was thrown forward as her car collided with an enormous, ancient oak tree—she had looked over her shoulder at the wrong moment and had driven straight through a bend in the road and right into the forest. Her head struck the windshield and blood ran into her eyes as her vision wavered and darkened. Agony rushed through her entire body, and she gasped as she struggled to catch her breath.

The engine ticked as it cooled and smoke rose in dark, snaky wisps from underneath the crushed hood. Kayla groaned and blinked, but instead of becoming clearer her vision grew darker. She couldn't think past the crushing agony in her head. She fumbled for her cell phone before remembering that she'd left it at home.

God, didn't I learn my lesson the last time I left my phone somewhere? I'm so stupid, she thought, thinking painfully of the day her father had died, when she'd left her phone in the truck.

She didn't know how much time passed; she was concentrating on simply staying conscious. It was a battle that she was quickly losing. She prayed that somebody would discover her soon, but nobody came to her aid.

Finally, she heard crunching footsteps outside the vehicle. Relief swept through her. She didn't know how much longer she'd be able to hold on; the blackness threatened to consume her more with each passing minute.

The door swung open and her relief rapidly turned to dismay and terror.

The blond man smiled at her. He was speaking, but Kayla didn't understand what he was saying; she finally lost her grip and she was plummeting down into darkness.

Chapter 9

The first thing she became aware of was her feet; she could feel the tips of her toes dragging against the ground. She was also aware of strong hands gripping both of her arms. Her head lolled against her shoulders, and her entire body was a symphony of pain. She could hear somebody panting and birds singing above her head.

She slowly opened her eyes. It took every ounce of strength she had in her.

Two men were half-carrying, half-supporting her as they walked down a narrow path. Trees surrounded them on all sides, and she observed the dim quality of the light. She was in the forest, and it was nearly dark.

She glanced at her captors, and with no surprise she saw that they were the two men from before. The third one, the blond man, was walking some distance ahead of them, picking his way through the trees with a demeanor of experience, as if he'd been down this path many times before.

"She's awake, William," one of the men called.

"Doesn't matter. We're almost there," he replied over his shoulder.

Kayla felt like death itself. Her pounding head and aching limbs wouldn't have allowed her to run away in any circumstance, and she knew that she had no chance of escaping the three men in her condition. But something that the man had said registered, and she frowned a little. The gesture hurt her face.

"Hang on," she muttered to herself. "William?" A creeping suspicion began to take hold of her.

The man on her left gripped her arm tighter, and she cried out a little as a bolt of pain shot through her arm. "Shut up," he instructed.

A building loomed into view ahead. Kayla gulped.

It was an enormous, white, three-story Victorian-style house. She supposed it was a very attractive building, but it looked extremely out of place in the middle of the dark, thick, oppressive forest.

The two men steered her forward as they followed William. He strode up to the front door and swung it open without even bothering to knock.

One of the men holding her kicked the door closed behind him, but they didn't follow William up the stairs; instead they waited in the hallway. Kayla glanced around nervously. It was dark inside the house, incredibly dark; she could barely see a thing. Although the house was clean, as far as she could see anyway, a thick smell of dust and age hung in the air.

She suspected that, with a house this old, there was no way to get rid of that smell.

The steely taste of terror filled her mouth. She hadn't told anyone where she was going. How on earth would Emerson and the rest of the pack ever find her? She cursed her own stupidity.

Footsteps, two sets of them, approached from the stairwell. William was coming back down the stairs, but this time he wasn't alone.

Kayla's eyes widened as her suspicions were finally confirmed. "You," she gasped.

Adam crossed his muscular tattooed arms but didn't reply as he stepped in front of her. "Let her go," he shot to the two men.

"But—"

"Do it," he commanded sharply, and the two men immediately released her arms, as if afraid of disobeying him. "It's not as if she's going anywhere."

"Where am I?"

Adam ignored her again. He circled around her, looking her up and down. He frowned and turned to William, who looked pleased.

"I did good, huh?"

"No, you didn't," Adam said quietly. His voice was calm and steady, but cold anger flickered across his face. "I told you not to hurt her." He nodded towards Kayla's bloody, bruised face.

"She did that to herself. She crashed her car into a tree," William retorted scornfully. He alone seemed immune to the effect that Adam seemed to have on the other two men.

Kayla was scared, beyond scared, but she willed herself to appear calm and in control. "Adam Harper," she said. "I was looking for you, you know."

Adam finally made eye contact with her. "Well, you found me," he said, raising his eyebrows. The two men laughed, but immediately fell silent when he held up his hand. "And why were you looking for me, exactly?"

She stared directly into his piercing blue eyes and willed herself not to look away. "I'll tell you when you tell me why you sent your pack to kidnap me."

"I see that your father's henchmen already told you our little secret," Adam said scathingly. His upper lip twitched.

"Answer the question." She didn't know where her sudden courage was coming from, but she was glad. She didn't want to appear weak.

Adam seemed to ponder her request, and to her surprise he nodded. He glanced at the other three men. "Go join the others, I'll talk to her."

William shot Adam a withering look, but he obeyed and stepped out of the hallway through a doorway. The other two men followed obediently.

"Follow me," Adam shot curtly over his shoulder as he turned around and strode towards the narrow, rickety stairwell. Kayla swallowed, considered dashing towards the door, then decided that trying to escape while four werewolves were nearby, was probably a bad idea. So she took a deep breath, tried to ignore her rising terror, and followed Adam.

He led her all the way to the top, to the third floor. The higher they climbed, the dustier and more neglected the house became. She sneezed as they stepped onto the third-floor landing. The chocolate-brown carpet was thick with dust.

He swung open a door on the left and stepped inside. Reluctantly, Kayla followed.

The room was much cleaner and more welcoming than she'd expected. It was spotlessly clean and free of the dust that plagued the rest of the third floor. There was a soft queen-sized bed, a large old-fashioned wardrobe, a writing desk, and an attached bathroom.

Adam turned to her and crossed his arms. "This is where you'll stay."

"Can't I go home?" she asked, her voice trembling slightly.

"You can't. Not yet." Was it her imagination, or did he sound slightly apologetic?

"Why not? What have I ever done to you?" she said. The note of accusation in her voice was crystal-clear, even to herself.

Anger flickered across his incredibly handsome face. "Don't test my patience." She flinched a little from the malicious snap in his voice. "You know exactly what this is about."

She crossed her arms, her heart pounding in her chest. Her face still hurt, incredibly so, but she ignored the pain. "All I know is that my father killed the man responsible for murdering my mother, the man who belonged to your pack. He might have been a little hot-tempered, but you can't blame him for wanting revenge. And I went looking for you because the rest of his pack—the pack that I'm in charge of now—want to kill you, and I was hoping that you and I could talk together and come up with some kind of solution. So yeah, you're attacking me because I wanted to save your life. I don't know about your logic, Adam."

All through her speech, Adam's handsome face had slackened, and his mouth opened slightly in surprise. He raised his eyebrows and let out a single humorless laugh. He shook his head.

"Oh my God. Is…" he laughed again, but it was incredulous and bitter, and Kayla's heart lurched unpleasantly. "Is that what your father told you? That the man who killed your mother was a member of *our* pack?"

A cold finger of disquiet touched Kayla's heart, and she shivered a little. "Yes," she said, forcing her voice to sound as strong as possible.

Adam finally stopped laughing, and he only looked angry again. He paced around the room, his mouth working soundlessly, and finally he burst into speech.

"Your mother's murderer was a man named Richard Long. He was a rogue shifter, a wolf with no pack. He drifted from town to town, never putting down roots in one place for long, and for good reason. He'd completely given in to his lupine side, rarely ever shifting back to a man, and his bloodlust and hunger were frightening to behold. He developed an appetite for human women."

Kayla swallowed. She felt cold all over, even though the room was warm. She didn't want Adam to continue, didn't want to hear any more about her mother.

"That was nine years ago, and my father was the alpha at the time. I was young, only sixteen, but I was his second-in-command." A note of pride entered his voice. "We'd gotten wind of Long's…activities, so to speak. We keep a close eye on the news, and we know the signs of a rogue shifter. He killed at least nine women, and it was clear from the trajectory of his victims' location that he was headed this way. We intended to intercept him here, on the outskirts of Lewiston, and put him down. It was only right. So my father and I, and ten others, shifted into our wolf forms and waited in the forest."

He paused, and his face changed, breaking out of its angry shell. His eyes were soft and apologetic. Something loosened in Kayla's chest.

"I'm sorry," he said gently. "We made a mistake. We assumed he would come in from the mountains. We never dreamed he would follow the roads; he didn't like human civilization. By the time we heard her screams and rushed to her aid, we were too late."

Kayla had to sit down on the edge of the bed; her legs felt weak.

"If it's any consolation at all, we killed him and stopped him from eating her body. At least you were able to bury her."

Something flickered in her mind, piercing through the haze of pain and confusion surrounding her mind.

"That's not right...my father said that he killed him."

Fury, pure fury, filled Adam's face, transforming it from handsome to something terrifying. "No. Your father murdered someone else. Landon Price, a member of my pack. One of my blood brothers. He was young, my age at the time. Just a kid, really. He was out on his own that day, scouting the forest. Your father saw him near the area that your mother was killed and jumped to conclusions. Landon didn't even have a chance to defend himself."

Kayla's face drained of color, and she felt as if she might puke.

"No," she whispered. Her husky voice cracked. "No, he wouldn't do that!"

"He did," Adam said shortly. "Grief had rendered him unreasonable and erratic. We knew that we couldn't reason with him, couldn't explain that your mother's murderer had already been caught." He was pacing extremely quickly now. "At the time, our pack was afraid of your father's, you see. Your great-grandfather's reputation as a shapeshifter warlord, the man who'd defeated the Bane so long ago, was enough to make my father think twice. Did we really want to start a war with Mark Hudson, the man whose veins ran thick and hot with the blood of the alpha? No. Landon had been an orphan with no blood relatives to fight for justice on his behalf. We mourned the kid, buried him, and hoped that Mark would be satisfied."

Kayla didn't want to hear any more. She'd heard far too much today. She wanted to sleep, to forget about everything, and to remember her father as he had been to her—a grumpy old man who liked to fish.

But neither could she pretend that Adam wasn't telling the truth. It was written all over his face. As much as she hated to admit it, she believed him.

"He seemed to move on, and we relaxed. Nobody else had to get hurt." He stopped and turned to face her. She gripped the sheets tighter in her clenched fists.

"But three years ago, your father somehow discovered that Landon had belonged to our pack. He was furious; he felt as if justice hadn't been served, and that we all had to pay for what he had lost.

"At that time I was alpha; my father had passed the mantle on to me a couple of years prior. I tried to reason with Mark, tried to explain that we put down your mother's murderer the night she was killed, and that Landon had been innocent." He paused. "He didn't believe me, of course. I can't entirely blame him for that; too much time had passed, of course it looked suspicious that I would tell him otherwise. He accused me and the rest of my pack of plotting your mother's murder. He declared war."

Kayla remained silent, hardly daring to breathe. She was full of questions, but she was afraid that if she opened her mouth she would get sick. Adam took advantage of her silence and continued; he almost seemed relieved to get it all out.

"Honestly, I could have ended it that day. We're young and strong, and there's so many of us. Your father's pack is old and weak, and we were reluctant to kill them outright—we could have obliterated them, but it would have been dishonorable. So I made the decision to play defense, so to speak. In his day, your father was a force to be reckoned with—but his old age and his self-righteous fury had dulled his mind and rendered him little more than a nuisance...or so we thought.

"He was stronger than I gave him credit for. He ignored my pleas for peace, ignored our unwillingness to fight back. He gathered his pack and launched several attacks on us. At first it was rather easy to rebuff them, but your father's pack was surprisingly...relentless." He rubbed the side of his face, and suddenly he looked much older. "Last year your father seriously injured Paul, William's younger brother. He nearly died."

Something clicked into place in Kayla's mind. "Is that why William seems upset with you?"

Adam smiled grimly. "You picked up on that, huh?"

"Yeah."

"Yes, he's upset with me," Adam sighed, and despite her situation, Kayla felt a strong pang of sympathy for him. He wasn't quite the intimidating, ruthless killer that her father's pack had painted him to be. "As soon as it was clear that Paul was going to make a full recovery, William was all but foaming at the mouth. 'We've sat idly by for far too long,' he said. 'It's time for us to strike back, really strike back. They'll never know what hit them.'"

"And you wouldn't let him," Kayla guessed.

"Correct. I was still unwilling to kill the old wolves…even though I knew that that would be the outcome eventually. Since your father declared war, we really have no choice. The laws are clear, and although I never wanted to fight, I'll be damned if my brothers will be forced to leave their home."

"It doesn't have to be that way," Kayla insisted. Her eyes lit up with her plea. "Listen to me. This is all just a huge misunderstanding. I'm not trying to defend my father's actions, but I loved him and I still do. I knew him the most, and I know that he was just trying to do what was right. But now we have the chance to set it right, all of it. We can—"

"That's what I'm doing now," Adam said sharply, and suddenly Kayla was afraid again. "Making things right. I wish it hadn't had to come to this, but this is the best solution."

"What are you talking about?" A cold wave of fear washed through her. "Are you going to kill me?" Her mouth was uncomfortably dry and her lips were numb.

"No," Adam said quietly. He was looking at her oddly, almost sympathetically. "The laws state that you must die, yes, but it's vague. Since you weren't in this from the beginning, since you only found out about your father recently—yes, I can tell, this is all new to you, I can see it in your face—I don't think the law applies to you. You're not a shifter, and it's not as if you can actually fight us, after all."

"If you're not going to kill me, what are you going to do?"

Adam's jaw tightened. "Keep you here. The message has already been sent to Emerson, who for all intents and purposes is really in charge of your father's pack now. He's the honorary alpha, and it's him that we need to deal with."

"You're going to kill him?" Kayla cried as dread filled her heart.

"He was going to kill me," Adam pointed out, crossing his arms. "At least that's what you said. Thank you very much for the warning, although it was quite unnecessary."

"Please don't hurt him," Kayla whispered. "He's my uncle."

"I have to," Adam said in a dull, listless voice. "Then the rest of his pack will scatter and you and I can both go back to our old lives."

Kayla stared at him. Did he really believe that? She could never go back to the way it was before. Never.

"Don't worry," Adam said, and his voice sounded more natural now, less forced. "There's no need for you to get hurt, and that's a promise that I'm going to keep. As long as you stay here and don't try to escape or send a message to your uncle, you'll be okay."

"Wait!" she cried as Adam turned his back on her. He paused. "How long will it be?"

Adam pondered her question, then seemed to decide that there was no harm in divulging more information to her. "He will meet with us one week from now, in order to get you back. Either he'll give himself up without a fight or not."

"A week," she whispered to herself. It was hopeless.

Adam stopped with his hand on the doorknob, looking over his shoulder at her. His expression was strange, soft and gentle for a man holding her hostage. "I have to ask you not to leave this room, but I'll do everything in my power to make sure that you're comfortable here. And Kayla, I'm sorry that you had to get dragged into this."

With that, he exited the room, leaving Kayla with no company aside from her panic.

Chapter 10

She paced the room restlessly. She couldn't sleep. Part of the reason behind her sleepless state was, understandably enough, her fear—not for herself, but for the others. It boiled inside of her and sent alternatively hot and cold waves washing through her entire body.

The other part was the noise. It was hard to sleep when wolves kept howling in the forest outside of her window.

She peered through the lace curtains. As high up as she was, she could see them, dim shadows loping through the forest floor. It was nearly midnight, but the moon was full and cast an alabaster glow over the forest. She could see everything almost as clearly as she could in the daylight. It was a little eerie.

Most of Adam's pack was patrolling the forest; she assumed watching to ensure that her father's pack, and Emerson in particular, wouldn't show up. Or maybe that was what they were counting on.

She wondered how worried and afraid Emerson must be for her, and guilt caused her stomach to swoop. If only she hadn't been so stupid as to sneak out on her own, this wouldn't have happened.

It was hard for her to wrap her mind around the fact that, until this morning, she hadn't the faintest idea that werewolves were anything more than a myth. So much had happened in such a short amount of time, it felt as if a week or more had passed.

She took a deep breath and stopped her restless pacing. She decided that, as long as she was being held prisoner, she might as well try to be comfortable. She began to explore the room that would be her prison.

It wasn't that bad. It was large, spacious, and clean, and at least she had her own bathroom.

For about the tenth time, she half-heartedly tried to jiggle the doorknob. It was still securely locked. She wasn't so sure she wanted to get out, anyway. She didn't want to face the wrath of thirty angry werewolves.

She was still way too keyed up to sleep, so she decided to at least get a shower and feel half-human again. She swung open the large antique wardrobe and her eyes flew open with surprise.

It was fully stocked with expensive-looking clothes, all in her size by the look of them; dresses, frilly skirts, fashionably faded jeans, and blouses. She noted that they all still bore tags. Brand-new clothes? She glanced at one of the tags and gasped. Expensive indeed. She hadn't even paid that much for her used car.

She glowered at the clothes. If Adam thought that a few pricey outfits would make up for kidnapping her, he was sorely mistaken.

It was kind of touching, though.

There were no pajamas, only a lacy nightgown. She grimaced, but finally her urge to change out of her dirty, blood-stained clothes won out.

She examined her face in the bedroom mirror. The cut on her forehead had dried to an unsightly scab, but it wasn't nearly as deep as she'd feared. Her head still hurt, but she didn't think she had a concussion—she assumed she'd probably passed out from shock, mostly, after crashing her car. Her whole body ached, though, and her face was bruised.

After a long, hot bath in the Jacuzzi-style bathtub, which was big enough to hold at least eight other people, she dressed in the flimsy nightgown and sat on the edge of the bed.

She stared at the wall, puzzled. Why had Adam gone through all this trouble to make sure she was comfortable? Why did he care? She was the enemy.

A knock at the door startled her. Without waiting for a response, a key scraped at the lock and the door swung open.

"I thought you might be hungry," Adam said. In his hands, he balanced a tray laden with the most delicious-looking food Kayla had ever seen outside of a restaurant. Her stomach growled, but she refused to cave; she crossed her arms in front of her chest, a gesture of defiance as well as modesty, and glared in the opposite direction.

Adam set the tray on her bedside table with a loud clatter, and he sighed. "Please don't be difficult."

Although there was nothing remotely funny about the situation, she laughed. A muscle jumped in Adam's jaw.

"You're holding me hostage and planning to kill my uncle and I'm being unreasonable because I won't look at you?" she retorted.

He sighed again, and he sounded so defeated that Kayla was caught by surprise, and she glanced at him, the hostility draining from her face.

He closed the door and, after making sure that it was securely locked, sat down on the bed beside her. Against her will, her heart began to race. His scent was intoxicating—a rich combination of cologne and an earthy, masculine smell that she couldn't quite place. And he was incredibly handsome, of course…and dangerous. She would do well to never forget that Adam was dangerous.

He rubbed his forehead and closed his eyes. "I love each and every member of my pack like they're my brothers. In all ways but blood, they are. Can you believe that?"

She blinked, took in the sheer sincerity of Adam's tone and his face, and nodded. "Yes, I do."

"Then can you understand how painful it was to me, as their leader, to stand aside in the face of danger? I felt like a coward; worse, I felt like the enemy. My brothers were getting hurt, and my pride and dignity meant nothing. But more than that…

"Can you keep a secret?"

She rolled her eyes, but she was inwardly dismayed at how her guard seemed to be lowering around the sexy, mysterious alpha. "Of course. Who am I going to tell?"

He laughed a little at that. "True." He frowned a little, appearing to be deep in thought. "More than that, though…for some time now my second-in-command has been getting exceedingly restless."

"William?"

"Yes." His hands tightened into fists, although he didn't appear angry—he only looked sad. "William has been itching to take control of the pack and take my place as alpha. You see, William isn't just my second-in-command; he's also my cousin. Per shapeshifter law, he would technically be able to take the title from me. Ever since your father first declared war, relations between William and me have grown…well, tense. We used to be extremely close. Out of all of my wolf brothers, he'd always been my favorite. But the war has turned him bloodthirsty and callous, even more so since his brother's injury. He thinks I'm weak, you see."

"I don't think you're weak," Kayla said automatically. How strange it was for her to be defending her captor! But she meant it, just the same.

He raised his eyebrows. "Really?"

"Really," she repeated. "I think you're mature enough to understand that not all fights have to end in violence, and that you care deeply about your pack's safety—so much, in fact, that you're not willing to needlessly throw them into harm's way. And I think that, as much trouble as my father caused you, you respected him and his pack. There's nothing weak or shameful about that."

He nodded stiffly. "I suppose you're right. But William thinks otherwise. Sometimes I believe him. Mostly, though, I stick by my decisions."

"They're good ones. Except for the decision to kidnap me, of course."

She said it semi-jokingly, but to her surprise Adam's jaw tightened again. "It wasn't my decision." He glanced at her open-mouthed expression and nodded.

"William forced my hand. He holds almost as much power in the pack as I do, and after hearing of your father's death he was certain that Mark's pack would seize the opportunity to attack us. I can see now that he was right." He ran his hands through his thick, dark hair. "He thought that now was the time for action. He wanted to kill you outright, but I put my foot down on that one, and after a long, arduous argument we were able to come to this compromise. One of our laws is that no innocent humans should ever be killed. He was not convinced of your innocence. I was."

"How? You don't even know me. For all you knew, I could have been planning to attack you, too," Kayla pointed out, although after learning the unpleasant alternative to her kidnapping, she was deeply grateful to Adam for fighting for her life. Next to certain death, being imprisoned didn't seem quite so bad anymore.

He smiled a little at that, and her heart leapt in her throat. "Call it intuition, then. I think I was right."

"You were," she agreed grudgingly.

"Anyway," Adam continued with a small, troubled frown, "I know it's hardly appropriate to discuss my pack problems with you, but as you said before, it's not as if you're going to tell anyone. Besides," he added, not quite looking in her direction, "I find it pretty damn easy to talk to you."

Kayla was taken aback at that, but she retaliated quickly. "It's not like I have any choice but to listen."

She expected him to scowl, but he only looked weary. "Yeah. I know."

Although it was disquieting to think so, Kayla found, to her surprise, that she didn't like seeing Adam upset. She cleared her throat pointedly and changed the subject.

"So is this…I don't know…your base, I guess?"

"It's our den," he said, and again just the barest hint of pride entered his voice. "Most of us live here full-time. Of course from time to time we still interact with the human world, if only to keep up the charade. It hasn't been easy hiding a pack this big from the humans, but this place is perfect. It's on private land, you know, so nobody can enter without permission aside from the game warden and law enforcement—and they're already in on the secret, so they respectfully keep their distance."

"Wow," she said, impressed against her will. This pack seemed much more organized than her father's.

"Yeah, it's great. It's been in my family for over a hundred years. Only when my father became alpha did he get the idea to fix it up and use it as our den. We're far enough away from humans for privacy, but close enough to them to help if they ever need it."

"Do you do that a lot? Help humans?"

"As much as we can. Sometimes other shifters are a threat, of course, but we also protect them against wild animals and, if we get wind of it in time, other humans."

Kayla didn't answer at first; she only stared at the rug without really seeing it.

Again her perspective was being forced to shift. She didn't like it. She wanted to go on thinking that Adam and his pack were bloodthirsty killers, not protectors of the town. It would make her situation easier to deal with if she could believe that.

***

If Kayla had been aware that she was going to be kidnapped, she would have imagined a much different experience.

Over the next five days, Adam drifted in and out of her room as he pleased; sometimes to bring her food, more often to talk. She slowly began to realize that, as incredible as it seemed, despite the sheer number of people in his pack, Adam was lonely.

At first, she took his interest in her well-being and his constant company as a sign of his guilt; however, as the days slowly slipped past, she began to suspect a different motive—he truly cared about her comfort and safety, and he was genuinely sorry for the measures that he'd been forced to take.

He talked about all manner of things; mostly his pack, but he divulged a little about his upbringing and his family; about his father, the alpha before him, and his mother, both of whom had passed away. With a jolt of understanding, she'd realized that Adam knew exactly what she was going through. He'd lost both of his parents too.

Soon, she cautiously began to speak about her own life as well; about how she'd run away to college to escape her father, and how she was so glad that she'd come back. During those conversations she heavily hinted at her father's personality—how he really wasn't a bad guy, and how much he'd loved his family. Whenever she brought up Mark, Adam's jaw would lock tight and he would refuse to speak, so eventually she gave up on the topic.

After the third day, Adam had finally given in to her pleas and, after extracting a promise from her that she wouldn't try to escape, had allowed her to explore the rest of the house. Soon she was free to come and go from any room in the house as she pleased, a welcome respite from the cramped confines of the upstairs bedroom.

She was able to meet the rest of Adam's pack. Although some of them, acknowledging that she was the enemy, refused to speak to her, most of the other shapeshifters seemed to share Adam's views and welcomed her warmly. Although the atmosphere was dampened a bit by the unspoken fact that she was a prisoner in their home, she began to relax as she got to know the individual members of the Lewiston wolf pack.

She had no idea that they would be so... *brotherly*. Brotherly, loyal, and fiercely protective of each other. It could get rowdy in the house, of course—with thirty men in one dwelling, it would have been a shock if the testosterone hadn't manifested itself in some way—but the general sense of comradery and brotherhood never faded. She envied them a little.

It would have been easy to feel at home, if not for the fact that sometimes, with a jolt of shock, she would remember that the men that she was slowly growing attached to were planning on killing her uncle.

There was only one shifter amongst the pack who made her feel truly uneasy. William Burkhart never joined in any of the raucous conversations when she was in the room; instead he would lurk in the shadows, shooting malicious, hate-filled glances her way. They sent icy shivers down her spine.

Sometimes, if she was alone in a room, she would catch a quick flickering movement out of the corner of her eye and would turn to see William darting through the doorway...as if she'd caught him watching her.

She wasn't sure if she should say anything to Adam. William was the second-in-command after all, and she already knew he was unhappy that Adam had forced him to leave her alive. But she believed Adam when he said that she was perfectly safe in the wolves' den, and she decided that even if William truly wanted to harm her, he wouldn't dare go against a direct order from his alpha.

For the most part, she was happy and content...during the daytime. But at night, her terror for her father's pack cut her heart like a razor blade, and more often than not she would cry herself to sleep, pressing her face into her soft down pillow until it was soaked with her tears.

In the early hours of the sixth morning of her imprisonment, Kayla lay on her side, clutching her pillow close to her. Her eyes were dry, but her face was pale and drawn. Although it was past two in the morning, she couldn't sleep a wink. She hadn't even bothered to change out of her day clothes and had collapsed on the bed as soon as she'd gotten back upstairs from dinner. She hadn't moved too much since.

Only one more day left, she thought with a pang. *A little more than twenty-four hours, and Emerson is coming to meet them. They're going to kill him.* Finally, the tears needled and stung her eyes, and she let them fall shamelessly. *It's all my fault.*

She didn't even move when someone knocked on the door, didn't even flinch at the sharp sound of knuckles on wood. She didn't bother to answer him, either. He'd come in anyway. He was the one with the key.

When the door swung open, she glanced up. It was Adam, as she knew it would be. However, she didn't expect his expression.

Pain and sorrow flickered across his handsome, rugged face, and she sat up.

"I'm sorry," he said simply.

She didn't say a word, simply patted the bedspread. He sat down beside her on the bed, as he always did when he visited, but she had the distinct feeling that this time was different. He opened his mouth and closed it several times, as if he wanted to speak. Finally, he found his words.

"I can't stand this anymore."

She raised her eyebrows. "Stand what?" Her voice came out in a hollow, choked whisper.

"Everything," he said as he clenched his fists and stared in the opposite direction. "Keeping you here, for one. Letting William make all the major decisions, for another. The last thing I wanted was to lose sight of who I was, who the pack was. But kidnapping? That's not who we are. I just wanted to avoid another death, but abducting you was wrong."

"It hasn't been that bad," she allowed. She wondered why she kept doing this, kept defending him from himself. "The pack's been really good to me. I think that, in any other situation, I could be friends with them."

He glanced at her, his face drawn and hard. "That would be like a friendship between a prisoner and her guards. That's not right and it's not healthy."

She blew a sigh. "I don't know what to say, Adam. But you're not the bad guys. I really believe that."

He gave her an odd look. "I used to think that, too. Now I'm not so sure." He looked her in the eyes, and her stomach squirmed pleasantly. "There's something else."

"What is it?"

"I…well, I really don't know how to say it." He laughed a little. "There's something about you, Kayla. Something that's brought me back here to this room to talk to you time and time again even though I know better. I ought to have stayed away."

"I'm glad you didn't." And she meant it. Adam's company had meant everything to her.

"Just the same, I should have. But I couldn't." His eyes searched her face. "If not for the circumstances…I'd really like to know you better. In every way, in fact. I have feelings for you, Kayla, strong feelings, feelings I shouldn't have for someone

I've only known for a few days. If only the circumstances were different—"

"To hell with the circumstances," Kayla interrupted. She didn't know where her boldness was coming from, and she knew she should feel nothing but hatred and contempt for her captor, but she couldn't bring herself to hate Adam. He was strong and sensitive and handsome, and overall a good man. Her father had been wrong about him. She didn't think and didn't try to stop herself, even though her conscious mind knew that it was probably a mistake.

She leaned forward on the bed and kissed him. His eyes widened with surprise, but it only lasted a moment; he pulled her against him and returned the kiss. She melted against his muscular, rock-hard body, and when he swept his hot tongue across her lush, full bottom lip, she gasped.

She wrapped her hands in his thick dark hair and pulled his face closer, relishing every kiss and his warmth.

Finally, after what seemed like no time at all, he gently pulled away. She pouted, unsatisfied, but he stood up. She hesitated, wondering if she might have upset him somehow, but he was smiling a little.

"Thank you."

"For what?" Her entire body tingled with the warm rush the kissing had given her, and she wanted more—she wanted all of him. All rational thought had flown out the window, and she thought that it might be a blessing.

"For making up my mind for me." He glanced out of the window and frowned at the still-dark sky. "If you're tired you can go back to bed and we can go in the morning, but it might make more sense to go now."

"I'm not tired," Kayla answered truthfully. "And go where?"

"To take you home. I'm not doing this anymore. We'll figure something else out with your pack, but I'm never stooping so low as to take hostages ever again."

Her jaw dropped. She tried to speak but couldn't. Finally, she managed to say, "I'm free? I can go?"

He smiled. She thought that there was just the slightest hint of sadness to it. "Yes, you can go."

"What about William?"

His smiled faltered. "He'll be angry, but let me worry about that. He may hold power in the pack, but I'm still the alpha. Whatever I say goes."

She hesitated, torn. Part of her was desperate to return home to Emerson and the old, familiar comfort of her father's cabin. The other part of her wanted to stay here with Adam and his pack.

But if she did that, wouldn't she be joining the enemy? Would she inadvertently be destroying her father's old pack?

She couldn't do that. She couldn't turn her back on Emerson and everyone else who needed her.

"Thank you," she said sincerely. She crossed the distance between them and embraced him, trying to convey some of her gratitude in the gesture. "Thank you so much."

He stroked her hair for a moment, then released her. He tried to smile, but it looked sad and strained. "Come on. We'd better leave now."

"How are we going?"

He chuckled. "Unfortunately your car was pretty much totaled. You must have been going pretty fast. We towed it back here and stored it in the garage, but there's no way it's going anywhere anytime soon. I have a spare car you can use. I'll ride with you as far as the Youngstown town limit, then I'll get out and let you drive the rest of the way by yourself. It's not safe for me to be any closer to your father's territory right now; I'm sure your father's pack is out for blood."

"I wouldn't let them hurt you."

His eyes narrowed. "I'm not worried about that. If it came down to a fight between me and any one of those old wolves, I wouldn't lose. I just don't want to hurt any of them in front of you."

She glanced down at her feet. "Thank you, Adam," she repeated. She looked back into his eyes and hesitated before asking the question that was haunting her. "Is there a chance that we can see each other again after?"

"I don't know," he said slowly. "It's going to be rather impractical, isn't it, with both of our packs at war?" He saw her stricken expression and squeezed her hands. "Let's just concentrate on one thing at a time, and we'll take the rest as it comes. Let's get you home first."

"All right."

She gave the room that had been both her prison and her happy place one last sweeping glance before following Adam down the stairs. The house was dark and silent; no snores from sleeping men resounded behind the closed bedroom doors. She could only assume that, with the day of the handoff so close at hand, nobody else could sleep either.

"Almost there," Adam murmured.

"Have you told the rest of the pack?" she whispered back.

"No. I'll let them know in the morning. Most of them will stand behind my decision. They like you, you know," he replied in a low voice.

They reached the bottom of the stairs, and the front door was in sight. Kayla held on to Adam's arm and let him lead her through the narrow hallway; it was pitch-black and he had better eyesight than her, it seemed. But also she was uneasy. A chill that had nothing to do with the temperature ran down her spine.

As Adam's hand settled on the doorknob, the lights flicked on and Kayla squinted. She and Adam both spun around.

"I knew you'd cave," William said in a voice that was simultaneously menacing and disgusted. He was leaning against an open doorway, his blond hair hanging in his fierce, haunted eyes. He shot a look of pure loathing in Kayla's direction and approached them. Adam instinctively pulled Kayla behind him.

With a crashing wave of fear, Kayla saw the three huge, snarling wolves that loped out of the doorway and stopped at William's side.

Chapter 11

"I'm calling off the plan, William. I'm taking her home," Adam said sharply. There was no fear in his voice; only the loud ring of authority.

Fury glinted in William's eyes and one of the wolves let out an alarming growl. "I knew you were too weak to go through with it. What comes next, Adam? Surrender? If you hand her back over, you'll only prove to them that you've given up."

"I'm doing the right thing," Adam retorted. He pulled Kayla closer to his back as one of the wolves took a step forward.

"You're doing the cowardly thing," William corrected. "If you're not willing to lead this pack to victory, then I guess I'll have to."

For the first time, cold anger entered Adam's voice. "And how will you do that? Kill her? I won't let you."

"Your days of ordering me around are over," William snarled. "You've gotten complacent. Look at you! Putting the well-being of a *human* over the needs of the pack."

"It's our duty and responsibility to help people."

"Yeah, so you've said. You and your father and his father before him. You're all wrong." William's eyes gleamed, and at that moment Kayla's fear deepened. He wasn't just cold and callous. She feared he might also be mad. "Shifters are on the verge of extinction, thanks to humans. So why should we bend over backwards to help them?"

Adam was staring at William as if seeing him clearly for the first time. Sorrow and disgust warred on his face. "So this is it? You want to take over the pack?"

"If you don't step down, I'll take the title of alpha myself." The three wolves beside William snarled. "Cooper, Tyler, and Payton agree with me."

Adam snorted, but the incredulous gesture did nothing to hide the pain of his second-in-command's betrayal shining in his eyes. "And what about the rest of the pack? Do they agree?"

William's eyes narrowed. "No."

"And your plan is to attack me here, in the middle of the den? Even if you do manage to kill me, I don't think the rest of the pack would take that very kindly."

Triumph gleamed in William's eyes. "It doesn't matter, because they're not here. They can't intervene. I sent them off to patrol the forest; I fed them a bogus story and they all believed me. By the time they return, you'll be dead and they'll have no choice but to obey me."

Kayla was shaking. She held onto Adam's arms tighter. She was afraid—not for herself, but for Adam. She had no doubt that he was strong, but four against one? He didn't have much of a chance.

"You were like a brother to me," Adam said. His voice was soft and disarming. "We share the same blood. I trusted you. Can you really turn your back on blood so easily?"

William's hard expression faltered slightly, but the mask of anger returned. "You're the one who turned his back on me by choosing the well-being of the enemy over his own pack. Blood doesn't matter anymore. You're not fit to be the lowest-ranking wolf, let alone the alpha."

"I have a very different idea of who's not fit to be alpha," Adam said through gritted teeth.

William's upper lip twitched in a snarl. The moment was near; Kayla could feel the tension gathering in the air and crackling like an electrical storm. The three wolves crouched, their golden eyes gleaming with hatred and malice.

"Last chance," William said as he flexed his arms threateningly. "Hand her over and let me dispose of her, and issue the order to attack the Youngstown pack immediately, and I'll walk away right now. You can remain alpha and you might even regain my respect."

Kayla glanced at Adam's face. Part of her was worried that he would accept William's offer.

"No," Adam said firmly.

William's face was impassive as he replied, "I'm sorry then, *cousin*." The last word dripped sarcasm.

Everything happened so quickly, within a space of just a few seconds, but Kayla's terror seemed to slow down time, and she saw everything.

The same strange, blinding light that she'd seen surrounding Emerson when he'd shifted now filled the entryway, obscuring both William and Adam from view. Kayla stumbled backwards and pressed herself against the door as a strangled whimper burst from her lips.

When it faded, two wolves stood in the men's place—a huge, sandy-colored wolf hunkered down, snarling, where William had been just a second before, and now directly in front of Kayla, crouched down in a protective stance, was an even larger wolf. Adam's fur was brilliantly white and shaggy, and he towered over all of the other wolves, even William.

The other three wolves hesitated, fear shining in their eyes, but the sandy-colored wolf did not—William sprang at Adam, his white dagger-like teeth shining in the feeble glow of the overhead light. Adam tensed his body and met the other wolf midair. The floor under Kayla's feet shook with the impact.

She'd never seen anything like it as the two werewolves tumbled on the floor, biting and kicking and snarling. The hairs on the back of her neck lifted. She knew that she was witnessing something possibly as rare as a lunar eclipse—two very powerful wolf shifters fighting for control of their pack. It was raw and primal, and she knew that she would probably never see anything like it again as long as she lived.

William had the power of rage on his side, but even his anger-fueled strength had nothing on Adam's superior size and his desire to protect Kayla. William tried to break away and go straight for her, but Adam, with a growl that was more like a roar, tackled his cousin and chased after him when William ducked away with his tail between his legs.

But Kayla's heart sank as the other three wolves, who had been hovering indecisively in the background, sprang towards her. Adam let out a howl of frustration as he realized William's trick; he'd meant for Adam to go after him and leave Kayla exposed.

The three huge wolves were nearly upon her, all flashing teeth and shining eyes, and Kayla's blood ran cold. She was going to die.

Adam streaked away from William, his claws skittering on the hardwood, and overtook the lead wolf just as he reached Kayla. Adam's massive jaws locked onto the wolf's throat.

Between Two Packs

It was over in seconds; the wolf's blood spurted everywhere, splashing Kayla in the hot liquid, as Adam ripped out his throat. The wolf collapsed, and Adam let out a howl of victory. Kayla gasped as she pressed herself closer against the door; she thought she might be sick.

The two remaining wolves retreated to William's side, whining. The second-in-command's eyes narrowed. He yipped once and swept his tail from side to side. It seemed to be a signal, for at that moment all three wolves leapt towards Adam.

Before that moment Kayla had never really feared that Adam would lose; now, however, with three wolves on top of him, biting and clawing and snarling, she wasn't so sure. The sharp smell of blood stung her nose as the furious battle waged in front of her.

Adam flung one of the wolves away from him, but the other two circled, darting in and sinking their ivory teeth into his flesh and darting away again. His snarls of rage turned into ones of pain, and his efforts were growing weaker as he changed his approach; instead of attacking, he attempted to defend himself from the relentless wolves.

She had to do something. She'd never felt so helpless in her life. The thought of losing Adam sparked in her a fear far greater than the thought of dying. The two wolves pinned Adam to the ground. His throat was exposed, and William bared his teeth in what appeared to be a triumphant smile.

As he prepared to dart in for the kill, instinct took over. She didn't know where her sudden bravery came from, but it seemed to surge inside of her like a red-hot wave. She lunged forward, crossing the distance in just a handful of steps, and intercepted the sandy-colored wolf just as he was about to pounce. She shoved him as hard as she could with both hands, using his forward momentum and his compromised balance against him; even though she wasn't very strong, the wolf was sent flying away from Adam.

But he didn't stay down for long; her heart leapt in her throat as she realized that all she'd really done was anger him. William stood up, shaking with rage as his eyes locked with hers. She was in between him and Adam, who was desperately trying to get to his feet but still impeded by the other two wolves, but that didn't matter. He wanted to kill her just as badly as he wanted to kill Adam, and she'd presented him with an easy target.

He lunged, his teeth bared. She didn't have time to react, and her feet felt as if they were encased in cement. She stood rooted to the spot, certain that she was about to die.

She was knocked over with the force of the brute's body. Her head struck the hard wooden floor, and her vision doubled. The wind was cruelly knocked out of her lungs, and sharp, white-hot pain flared in her ankle; she supposed she might have twisted it or even broken it when she fell.

The wolf's hot, rancid breath filled her nostrils as the beast parted its jaws. She was pinned down and unable to move; she struggled, her eyes wide with terror. Behind her she heard Adam howling with frustration.

Her arm exploded in a fiery lake of pain as the wolf's jaws clamped on her right below her shoulder. She felt rather than heard her bone splinter as its fangs settled deeper into her flesh. It was pain unlike anything she ever felt before in her life. She tried to scream but couldn't.

Yips of agony sounded behind her. She couldn't turn her head, couldn't see which wolf was being hurt.

A furry white blur hit William, knocking him off her. Kayla sucked in a deep breath; her head had been spinning from the lack of oxygen. She lolled her head to the side and was greeted with the sight of the two gray wolves lying lifeless on the ground. Their bulging eyes were glassy and sightless.

Her vision was fading fast, but before she succumbed to the blackness, she watched as Adam darted forward and sank his teeth into William's throat.

***

She regained consciousness a little at a time. The first thing she became aware of was soft, mumbling voices, all male, drifting around her. Slamming doors. Footsteps. The sharp, stinging smell of antiseptic.

The second thing she acknowledged was the pain; it was dull, as if the pain itself had been wrapped in cotton and buried down deep inside of her. It was there, but it was tolerable.

The third thing she noticed was how warm and comfortable the bed was. Her eyes were still closed, and she would have been content to drift off back to sleep, but fear surged inside her as she remembered the battle and her eyes popped open again.

People, at least ten of them, surrounded her bed. She recognized them as members of Adam's pack. Relief flickered across their faces.

"You're awake," one of the men said. "Good."

"You're okay," a voice murmured from her right. Kayla turned her head and a deep, aching relief washed through her. Scratches covered Adam's hands, arms, and face, and a blood-stained bandage was wrapped around his head, but he was alive.

"What happened?" she managed to ask.

"Your ankle is sprained and your arm is broken," Adam said as he gently took her hand, "but you'll live.

Theo here," he said, nodding at a handsome blond man leaning casually in the doorframe, "works part-time at the hospital in the city. He's our makeshift doctor whenever we need him. His cover gives him access to all kinds of medicines and stuff. He gave you some morphine, set your arm, and stitched up your bites. They were deep, all the way to the bone; you needed a lot of stitches."

She tried to thank Theo, but she could barely speak above a whisper, and her thoughts were fuzzy and unfocused. He seemed to get the message, however. "You're welcome. Just make sure you keep off that ankle for a while."

Adam helped her drink some water, and after he set the glass down on the nightstand Kayla asked, "What happened to William?"

The men standing around her bed narrowed their eyes, and one of them cursed under his breath. Adam's eyes hardened. "I killed him."

"Oh, Adam," she whispered. "I'm so sorry."

"Don't be," he said roughly. "He chose his own fate."

Kayla was silent. She studied Adam's face. She knew that Adam wouldn't regret killing William, but she observed the deep sorrow in his eyes and knew that it would be some time before he got over his cousin's betrayal and his death.

Kayla rubbed her eyes. The morphine in her system was definitely doing its job. She wanted to ask Adam what came next, but before she could, she drifted off into a deep, dreamless sleep.

Chapter 12

"How are you feeling? Are you in pain?" Adam asked anxiously.

Kayla struggled to hide her grimace as she slowly sat up. She was in pain, a great deal of it—her arm felt as if it were on fire and there was a deep-set itch in her bones, one that was slowly driving her crazy. But she didn't want to worry Adam. Her eyes flickered over to him, and she decided to lie.

"No, not really. My arm itches really bad, though."

He frowned. He didn't seem convinced. "Well, you should take it easy, at least. If you want to stay in bed for another day—"

"Nuh-uh. No way!" Kayla narrowed her eyes. "I'm getting up today."

Adam had put her on mandatory bed rest ever since her injury, and while she was sure that she probably needed to heal, she was bored out of her mind. The TV reception sucked, and she'd already read every book Adam had brought her. There was nothing to do but stare at the ceiling and twiddle her thumbs. Adam made excellent company, it was true, but she longed to stretch her legs.

Adam's eyebrows creased, and he seemed to be thinking hard. Finally, he nodded. "Okay. I'll help you."

He took her uninjured arm and gently helped her sit up. Kayla gritted her teeth, determined not to let her pain show. She was sore all over.

"Can you stand?"

"I think so."

He helped her to her feet and she carefully tried to put some weight on her ankle. To her surprise, it wasn't that bad. She could walk, as long as she hobbled a little.

"Can we go downstairs?"

"Sure. Just be careful."

She leaned against Adam's hard, muscular shoulder as they slowly made their way down the stairs. The house was deserted.

"So what happens next?" she asked as they made their way to the den. She eased onto the couch and leaned back, closing her eyes. The short trip had taken its toll on her weakened body; she was exhausted.

"What do you mean?"

She glanced at him. "What's going on with Emerson?"

He fidgeted a little. He looked uncomfortable. "I was wanting to wait until you've healed a little to tell you—"

"Tell me what?" she demanded. She sat up straighter, which sent a bolt of pain shooting down her arm. Adam looked simultaneously sheepish and anxious, and immediately she was suspicious.

"I sent a messenger to Emerson to tell him that the deal was off, but that you were in no condition to come home. We didn't tell him what had happened to you, obviously. But he's a very shrewd man, and it's clear that he knows something's not right. He's been sending us nasty messages, threatening to come up here and see you for himself. He's very concerned about you. We reassured him that you were okay, but he's not convinced."

Kayla felt a strong surge of affection for her uncle. "Of course he's not."

Adam glanced at her. A resigned sort of unhappiness shone in his eyes. "In another day or so, you should be okay to travel. We'll see you safely back home, as I originally planned. I don't know what's going to happen next. We're still at war with your...I mean, Emerson's pack. It's best if we go our separate ways."

Kayla swallowed. She should have been thrilled that she was free to go, but she wasn't. She didn't want to leave Adam. And oh, it wasn't fair. Why was she falling in love with him?

"I don't want to leave," she said firmly.

He locked eyes with her, incredulity clear on his face. "It's my fault you got hurt. If I'd known what William was capable of, or better, if I'd never allowed him to talk me into bringing you here in the first place—"

"Stop," she interrupted, touching Adam's lips with her fingertips. They were soft and smooth, like velvet, and with a shiver she remembered how they'd felt against hers. "It's not your fault."

"I don't believe that," he murmured.

"You can't blame yourself. You didn't make William attack me."

"I should have known," he said, a note of anguish entering his voice.

"He was a bully and a tyrant. You can't take responsibility for his actions!" she said, her voice raising in pitch until she was almost shouting.

Adam's eyes grew strange and glassy, too shiny almost, and he quickly glanced away. With a jolt of wonder, she realized that he was close to tears. He cleared his throat, but his voice was steady when he spoke. "I keep remembering the way he was, before he changed. When he was like my brother. I see him in my dreams sometimes." He finally looked at her again, and his eyes were dry this time. "I don't regret killing him, though. Anything to keep the pack...and you...safe."

She wanted to take away Adam's pain, wanted to reassure him. She leaned forward and pressed her lips against his. He sighed a little and kissed her back firmly.

"Kayla, this is wrong," he said when they finally pulled apart. He looked anguished again, torn. "I can't stay away from you, and I don't know why. But we can't be together."

Her heart plummeted to her knees, and now tears of her own threatened to sting her eyes. "Yes we can," she insisted weakly.

He chuckled darkly. "No, we can't."

She stared at the wall, her heart heavy with sorrow. "I don't want to leave," she whispered.

"I don't want you to, either."

They sat in silence on the sofa together. She got the sense that Adam was brooding, but she wasn't. She was scheming.

If only there was some way that she could be with Adam. The easiest way, of course, was to denounce her father's old pack, and her uncle, and join Adam, and stay here with him...if he would even want her to, that is.

But she couldn't bring herself to even entertain that option. She'd be abandoning her father's pack, turning her back on Emerson and her father's memory, and leaving them to whatever fate might come.

No, she needed something more, something that would do more than simply allow her and Adam to be together…

Before she could think, Adam swiftly stood up. "That's enough exercise for one day," he said firmly. "Let's get you back in bed."

She groaned.

***

That night, Kayla listened to the sounds drifting up from the stairs—laughing, shouting, clinking plates, and the television blaring some old sitcom. The pack was sitting down for supper at the enormous table in the dining room downstairs. She wanted to join them, but she was sure that Adam would protest. He'd bring her up a tray later, just like he had every day since her injury.

She scowled. She really wasn't in *that* much pain. Adam was just overprotective.

She glanced around. She'd insisted that Adam move her from the second-floor bedroom, which had been more convenient for the pack's doctor, up to her old bedroom, the one on the third floor. It was cozy and familiar, and she already thought of it fondly as hers.

She hobbled into the bathroom to get a shower, which ended up being a much more complicated affair than it should have been. It took her nearly forty-five minutes, and she had to stick her cast awkwardly out of the shower the entire time.

She combed and blow-dried her hair, brushed her teeth, and hobbled painfully to the bed before collapsing on the comforter. She'd overestimated her strength.

As soon as she laid down, somebody knocked on the door. Pleasure surged through her chest. "Come in," she called as she sat up and self-consciously adjusted her nightgown.

As she'd thought, it was Adam. He swung open the door and gently sat down beside her on the bed.

She immediately noticed that he must have gotten a shower, too. The powerful, masculine scent of aftershave hung around his face like a fine mist, and she breathed it in.

"Once again, I can't seem to stay away from you," he said. Resignation and amusement warred on his face.

"I'm not complaining," she said breathlessly.

"I should. I'm only delaying the inevitable," he said sadly.

She frowned, biting her lower lip. Her earlier thoughts came rushing back to her. There had to be a way...

And suddenly it came to her, in a single glorious stroke of inspiration.

"Adam," she said suddenly. "I know how we can be together *and* end the war."

"What?" he asked cautiously.

She took a deep breath and began to explain her plan to him. Anxiety gnawed at her heart, and when she finally finished, he looked surprised.

"That's a good idea," he said slowly, as if he were struggling to remain patient with her, "but even if Emerson would agree, both of the packs wouldn't go for it. Nothing like that has ever been done before!"

"So?" she asked impatiently. "That doesn't mean that it can't be done."

He sighed. "I don't want to disappoint you, Kayla, but it would never work. Emerson hates us, as does the rest of your father's pack. They think we're responsible—"

"So explain!" she said, exasperated. "The war was caused by my father's misunderstanding. So set it right."

"He'll never listen to us. And I'm not sure that my pack would be comfortable with it anyway."

"They have to do what you say, don't they?" she pointed out.

Instantly she knew that she'd made a mistake; Adam's eyes gleamed with anger, and he clenched his jaw. "I would never force my pack to do something that they don't agree with. I'm their leader, not their dictator. I'm not William."

"Of course you're not," she said, alarmed that Adam had taken her words the wrong way. She hastened to explain herself. "I just meant that, if you thought that it was the right thing to do, surely they'd come to agree, right?"

He seemed to relax a little. "I don't know. Maybe."

"Will you think about it?" she asked.

He hesitated.

"I'll come with you," she promised. She seized his hands. "When you meet up with Emerson. I'll talk to him and make him see."

Adam sighed. "All right. I'll talk to the pack tonight, see what they think. If they're okay with it, I'll set up a meeting with Emerson."

"Thank you," she said brightly. "This will work, I know it."

Adam didn't look too convinced, but his uncertainty did nothing to pop the shining bubble of hope in Kayla's heart.

Between Two Packs

It was going to work.

Chapter 13

"I'm really not sure about this," Adam repeated in a low voice for the third time.

Kayla squeezed his hand reassuringly. "It'll be okay."

"If you say so."

"Shouldn't he be here by now?" Adam asked as he glanced around the park. A couple holding hands drifted by on the concrete walk in front of them, and a group of kids were playing Frisbee in the grass, but otherwise the park was empty.

"He'll be here," Kayla said confidently.

Adam shifted uncomfortably on the park bench and sighed.

After an entire night of arguing, Adam's pack had finally agreed to accept Kayla's plan. That had been the easy part; she feared that Emerson would be much harder to convince. This morning she'd called him, and he'd been frantic with worry. After finally convincing him that she was okay, she'd persuaded him to meet up with herself and Adam in a safe, neutral location—hence the Youngstown city park. Emerson had been suspicious, but finally he'd agreed. She hadn't told him anything about her plan, and she wondered how he'd react.

"There he is now," Kayla said, sitting up straighter. Emerson approached them, alone. The concern on his face quickly turned to anger and confusion as he saw the two of them holding hands.

"Kayla—"

"Don't be mad," she pleaded as she stood up and met Emerson halfway. He shot Adam a look of pure hatred and refused to step any closer to the bench.

"Why shouldn't I be?" His eyes flickered to Kayla's cast, and the anger faded from his face. "I was so damn worried about you. What happened to you? Are you all right?"

"It's a long story, but yes, I'm fine."

He glanced at Adam again and his upper lip curled. "You going to tell me what he wants?"

"Yes. Please, sit down and we'll talk it out."

"I'm not talking to him." Emerson grasped her hand. "I wanted to come just to make sure you were safe. Now I'm taking you home."

She locked eyes with him. "I'm not going anywhere until you talk to Adam." Her voice changed, becoming more soothing. "Please trust me, Emerson. Please?"

He frowned, glanced over at Adam one last time, and sighed. He slipped his hands into the pockets of his jeans and nodded. "All right. Fine."

He slowly approached Adam, his eyes wary. Kayla trailed behind him, nervous. She hoped that Emerson would be reasonable. He was generally a level-headed man, but fear and anger could cloud anyone's judgement.

"I'm glad you could join us today, Emerson," Adam said. He stuck his hand out for Emerson to shake it, but when the other man only glared, he withdrew it.

"Enough with the pleasantries, Harper," Emerson said roughly. He crossed his arms. "Tell me everything. Why is Kayla still with you, even after you kidnapped her? Why is she hurt? And what's the purpose of you meeting me here?"

Adam's face was calm, and when Kayla joined him on the bench, he slipped his arm around her shoulders. She closed her eyes, comforted by his touch. "I promise that everything I'm about to tell you is the truth. You just have to promise to listen. It might hurt—everyone knows how close you were to Mark, and what I'm about to say might be taken as an insult to his memory, but you have to believe that I'm telling the truth."

And he told Emerson everything, starting with the death of Kayla's mother and Mark's murder of Landon Price. His voice was so steady and sincere, and as all of the facts were laid out in front of him, the stony anger in Emerson's expression slowly leaked away.

"We all wondered," he said slowly, surprising Kayla, "if Mark's retaliation was justified. He was so grief-stricken, you see. How could he have been sure that the man he killed was Gloria's murderer?" He shook his head slowly. "Not that we would have ever questioned Mark. He seemed so sure of himself, so eventually we accepted it. It was always in the back of my mind…" His eyes met Adam's again, and the ferocity had returned. "Why? Why didn't you tell him sooner?"

"That was my father's fault, not mine. He feared Mark, and he didn't want a war," Adam said firmly.

"And you think we did?" Emerson challenged.

"Mark certainly did, or he would have stood down."

"You don't know what Mark was thinking," Emerson growled at him. "You didn't know him. I did. That man was my brother. Do you know what it's like to lose a brother?"

Adam's expression hardened. "Maybe I do."

Emerson stared at Adam. The uncertainly on his face deeply shocked Kayla. "I still don't trust you," he said slowly. But he glanced away, his eyes distant. "But I can't deny that your version of things fills certain…well, certain holes in Mark's version." He faced them again, his eyes filled with pain. "I don't want to believe Mark was wrong. I don't want to believe that he killed an innocent man. But do I have a choice?"

"I'm sorry," Adam said. "I can only imagine the shock you're in right now. I can only assure you that it's the truth, and if only you can accept it, we can finally begin the journey of putting it all behind us."

The genuine quality of Adam's voice finally seemed to thaw Emerson.

"All right," he said, crossing his arms. "I believe you. But you kidnapped Kayla and planned to use her against us. You can't talk your way out of that one."

Adam rubbed the side of his face. "Maybe not, but I can explain."

Emerson listened while Adam talked. He explained William's plan, and how he'd regretted going along with it the instant that Kayla had been brought to his house. "So yes, you're right. That was my fault, in the sense that I was weak enough to allow my second-in-command to talk me into it."

"And you were going to kill me?" Emerson's face was impassive.

At this, Adam smiled. The tenseness in his posture seemed to ease a little. "If I remember correctly, your plan was to kill *me*. We both planned to kill each other, so I think that makes us even."

Emerson seemed to be fighting a smile of his own. "Yeah, I guess you're right."

Adam continued talking. He told Emerson how he'd come to care for Kayla a great deal, and how his heart had hurt to see her held prisoner. "I didn't realize I was falling in love with her until the end of that week," he said, surprising Kayla. Her heart filled with warmth, and she had to fight back tears. "And I swore to myself that I wouldn't continue holding her captive."

He finished by explaining William's ambush and Kayla's injuries. He skated over the details of William's death, and Kayla could see fresh pain flickering in his eyes before disappearing again.

Emerson sighed and rubbed his temples. "What a mess. It was easier to hate you before. Now I don't know what to do."

"I have a proposition," Adam said. He glanced at Kayla. "Well, actually, it was Kayla's idea."

Emerson looked at him warily. "I'm listening."

But Adam seemed to have trouble speaking, so Kayla took a deep breath and said, "A truce."

"That seems fairly reasonable," Emerson said, frowning. "But...isn't it shifter law that the two feuding packs have to fight until there's a clear victor?"

"Shifter law isn't exactly concrete," Adam pointed out. "I broke the laws just by allowing Kayla to live."

Emerson seemed to be deep in thought.

Finally, he nodded. "Okay," he said with a sigh. "Okay, we'll accept your truce. As much as Mark would hate me for it, we won't fight you."

"Thank you," Adam said. "Don't you want to consult with your pack first?" Kayla didn't miss the emphasis on *your*. With a start, she realized that Emerson was the alpha now.

"No. I'm sure they'll agree with me, once I explain things to them. Truth be told, none of us really wanted to fight. We're too old, and without Mark to lead us, we were never really sure of a victory. And now that I know the facts, I could not in good conscience continue the fight that Mark started."

Kayla squealed with joy and leapt up, sweeping Emerson into a hug. "Thank you," she said breathlessly.

"For what?" Emerson asked, bemused, as he returned the hug.

She smiled up at him. "For my happiness," she said simply.

She wouldn't have to choose between her old family and Adam after all.

***

That night, she returned with Adam to his house in the forest. It was loud and raucous; the rest of the pack was celebrating the end of the war.

"Do you want to join them?" Adam asked as they lingered in the hallway.

Kayla shook her head. "No. I just want to get my stuff. I wouldn't be much fun tonight anyway. My arm hurts." She made a face.

"Are you looking forward to going back home?" Adam asked as he followed her up the stairs and into her bedroom.

She paused, in the process of packing up her clothes; Adam had insisted that she keep the clothes he'd bought for her. "No," she said finally with a sigh. "My only happy memories in that house came from my mother and my father. Now they're both gone." A pang of sorrow pierced her heart. "There's nothing for me there anymore."

Adam surprised her by pulling her into an embrace. Her heart raced as her hands traced his hard shoulders.

"I never officially asked you," he murmured into her ear. "Do you want to be with me? I'm not sure I could ever be enough for you, not for someone as beautiful, kind, and giving as you. But I promise that, if you would have me, that I'll give you everything that I have to give. I'll make you happy. I love you, Kayla. I never thought I could fall for somebody as quickly and as hard as I fell for you."

She gazed into his eyes, burning with the intensity of his statement.

"I love you too," she whispered.

When they kissed, Kayla thought she'd never been this happy in her entire life.

Epilogue

One month later

Kayla sat up and slowly stretched as the last fragments of her dream began to dissipate. It was a wonderful dream, one she'd had often since she'd begun staying the night with Adam in his den. She could never completely remember it, she only knew that it was a sweet dream and she always felt warm and happy once she woke up from it.

She pushed a lock of hair out of her eyes and glanced beside her. Adam's side of the bed was empty. She wasn't surprised; he was an early riser.

A slow smile stretched her lips and heat rose to her cheeks as she remembered the night before. Adam never disappointed her.

She climbed out of bed and slowly began to dress, being careful not to bump her cast. Her sprained ankle had healed quickly, but Theo had warned her that her arm would take much longer to heal. She hoped that she would be able to remove the cast too. Her arm no longer hurt, but it itched something awful.

The smell of bacon wafted up the stairs, and her stomach growled. She decided to go downstairs and grab some breakfast before the rest of the pack woke up.

She gave her reflection in the mirror one last sweeping glance before leaving the room.

She made her way to the kitchen, marveling at how different the house looked now. She didn't officially live here, but she spent nearly every waking moment at the den as well as most of her nights, and she'd put her own touches on the house. She'd decorated it and kept it spotlessly clean.

The kitchen was empty, and she quickly fixed herself a bowl of cereal and a glass of orange juice. When she was finished, she placed the dishes in the sink.

She wandered around aimlessly, wondering where Adam could be. It was a gorgeous morning—cool and clear. The birds trilled in the leafy canopy above her, and a squirrel scampered across her path. It was beautiful out here in the forest, and her heart swelled with contentment. She loved the house, she loved the people that she lived with, and above all else she loved Adam.

Finally, she picked up a sound coming from the shed behind the house. She made a beeline for it and stepped inside.

It was a huge building that was part storage and part garage. It was dusty and cluttered, but cozy nonetheless. In one corner of the building was her car, which Adam and two other men had been working on for a while now. It almost looked drivable.

The hood was popped open and Adam leaned over the engine as he examined it. He was shirtless, and Kayla's blood heated up as she raked her eyes across his muscular chest. They'd been together for a month now, but he still never failed to take her breath away.

"There you are," she called as she crossed the distance between them.

Adam's eyes lit up. He slammed the hood down, wiped his hands on his jeans, and swept her up in a hug, all while being careful of her cast.

"Just finishing up the transmission for you. You damaged it good, but give me just another day or two and I'll have it up and running."

She kissed him, marveling at the way his lips felt against hers. "Thank you."

"You're welcome," he murmured against her lips.

She leaned her head against his bare shoulder. "I'm so glad that everything worked out."

He held her tightly against his body. "Me too." He hesitated. "Kayla, are you happy here?"

"Are you kidding me?" she asked incredulously as she pulled away from him. "I haven't been this happy in a long time. I love it here."

He gave her a crooked little smile, what she always thought of as his special smile. "Good. I was afraid that, you know, after William you'd be afraid of us."

"Of course I'm not afraid of you guys."

"You're a remarkable woman, Kayla," he said.

Kayla shivered; it was the exact same thing her father had said about her mother. It was strange, like déjà vu, but sweet.

"I love you," she whispered as she gazed up into his handsome face.

"I love you too," he murmured.

As they kissed, she hoped that, if her father could see her now, he was finally at peace.

THE END

What to read next?

If you liked this book, you will also like *The Weekend Girlfriend*. Another interesting book is *Two Reasons to Be Single*.

The Weekend Girlfriend

Jessica has worked hard to be the paralegal that hotshot, sexy attorney Kyle needs. Unfortunately he doesn't see her as just his paralegal but also his own personal assistant. When he blames her for a mix-up in his personal life, Jessica sees no other option but to quit, thinking that her time with him is over. Much to her surprise, Kyle makes a proposition to her that she never thought she would hear coming from his lips. He needs a temporary girlfriend for his sister's wedding and he wants her to be that person. Jessica accepts the challenge and finds herself thrown into his world, learning things about him she never knew. The more time she spends with him outside of work, the more she is drawn to Kyle. As the wedding draws near, she finds herself fighting off some strong feelings for the man. When the wedding weekend is over, will Jessica be able to walk away from Kyle with her heart intact?

Two Reasons to Be Single

Olivia Parker has a job doing what she loves, a wonderful family and plenty of friends, but no luck in the love department. Tired of worrying about it, she decides to swear off love completely and focus on all the good things in her life. Just as she makes her firm resolution, Jake Harper arrives in town and knocks her plans into a tailspin. As the excited single ladies of Morning Glory surround the extremely attractive newcomer, Olivia steers clear of the "casserole brigade," as she calls the women, and tries to keep her distance from Jake. Instead, a variety of situations throw them together and they get to know each other better. They both have reasons for not wanting to get involved in a relationship, but the chemistry between them ignites, even as they desperately attempt to keep it at bay. As things heat up between Olivia and Jake, there is an aura of mystery about him that leaves Olivia certain that he is hiding something. When Jake disappears for a few days without telling Olivia that he is going out of town, she hates the way it makes her feel, and it reminds her of why she was giving up on dating in the first place. As Olivia's feelings for Jake grow, so does the need to find out what exactly brought him to Morning Glory and what he's been hiding.

About Emily Walters

Emily Walters lives in California with her beloved husband, three daughters, and two dogs. She began writing after high school, but it took her ten long years of writing for newspapers and magazines until she realized that fiction is her real passion. Emily likes to create a mental movie in her reader's mind about charismatic characters, their passionate relationships and interesting adventures. When she isn't writing romantic stories, she can be found reading a fiction book, jogging, or traveling with her family. She loves Starbucks, Matt Damon and Argentinian tango.

One Last Thing…

If you believe that *Between Two Packs* is worth sharing, would you spend a minute to let your friends know about it?

If this book lets them have a great time, they will be enormously grateful to you – as will I.

Emily

www.EmilyWaltersBooks.com

Made in the USA
Monee, IL
24 February 2022